"Who is she,

His black eyes searche[...]
Valentine," he said in a[...]
born on the fourteenth[...]

A muffled cry escaped Tracey's throat. "I mean her mother."

"She's our daughter, Tracey. Yours and mine."

"Our baby?" With fear and trembling, she took a long, hard look at the beautiful baby cradled in her lap. "No…" she whispered. How could she have given birth to Valentine and not known it, not remembered it? *How was that possible?*

"Now that you've met Valentine, you need to know everything so there won't be any more shocks."

"What do you mean more?"

"Raoul and Jules have been wanting to say hello to their mother for a very long time."

Dear Reader,

A special new delivery! We are proud to announce the birth of our new bouncing baby series! Each month we'll be bringing you your very own bundle of joy—a cute and delightful romance by one of your favorite authors. This series is all about the true labor of love—parenthood and how to survive it! Because, as our heroes and heroines are about to discover, two's company and three (or four...or five) is a family!

This month, it's the turn of award-winning author **Rebecca Winters** and an adorable set of triplets: *Three Little Miracles*, in fact. Next month's arrival will be (#3450) *His Brother's Child* by **Lucy Gordon**.

Happy Reading!

The Editors

Three Little Miracles
Rebecca Winters

Harlequin Books

TORONTO • NEW YORK • LONDON
AMSTERDAM • PARIS • SYDNEY • HAMBURG
STOCKHOLM • ATHENS • TOKYO • MILAN
MADRID • WARSAW • BUDAPEST • AUCKLAND

To Ronda,
whose baby twins provided
the inspiration for this book!

ISBN 0-373-03443-1

THREE LITTLE MIRACLES

First North American Publication 1997.

CHAPTER ONE

"GOOD morning, Tracey. How's our miracle patient today?"

Tracey paused in her writing to look up at her doctor. "Good morning, Louise."

"I'm glad to hear you call me by my first name."

The corners of Tracey's sculpted mouth turned up in a faint smile. "It seems an impertinence."

"Nonsense." Louise's keen eyes made a cursory examination. "You look good."

"I feel good. So good, in fact, that I'd like to go outside."

"All in due time," Louise murmured as she examined the latest entry in Tracey's journal. "Excellent. Your writing is as lucid and logical as I'm certain it was before your accident. You deserve a treat."

"I love treats."

"Good. Then you'll get one, but first, I'd like you to draw another picture for me."

Tracey stirred restlessly in the chair. "I'd rather play a card game or checkers with you."

"This is like a game."

"What do I have to draw?"

"You're still experiencing disturbing dreams about some kind of animal that terrifies you. I'm

5

curious to see what it looks like," she said, her eyes radiating compassion.

Tracey shook her head in denial and shrank from her.

"Come on, Tracey. You can do it. It's important. Maybe if I show you some pictures, you can tell me if any of them are the kind you keep talking about in your sleep."

Louise opened a book and flipped the pages slowly, urging Tracey to look. In spite of her fear, Tracey was fascinated by the dozens of animal pictures, everything from bighorn sheep in the wilds of the Yukon to gazelles roaming the darkest depths of Africa. When the last one appeared, Tracey lifted her head. "None of them looks like it."

Louise put paper and pencil in front of her. "I didn't think so. Therefore, I want you to draw what you continue to see in your mind. Remember, it can't possibly hurt you because it's only a picture on a piece of paper."

Tracey thought about it for a long time, trying to get up the courage. "If I do it this once, then will you let me go outside and walk on the grounds?"

"Tracey—I'm trying to get you well enough that you can walk out of here free to resume a full, productive life. But if you're so terrified of this animal, how can I let you go out of doors where animals live when a fear like yours is still unresolved?"

Letting out a tortured sigh, Tracey agreed, "You can't." After another long hesitation, she said, "All right. I—I'll do it. But I hate it." Her voice trembled.

With a less than steady hand, she began to draw the image of the horrifying creature that kept menacing her every time she closed her eyes and went to sleep.

No matter what she did, she couldn't hide from it. The only way to make it go away was to force herself to wake up. When she did, she found herself screaming and panting, completely exhausted. She'd discover that her body glistened with perspiration, that her pillow was drenched.

"There!"

She pushed the offensive drawing away. Louise picked it up without looking at it, then pulled out a wrapped chocolate bar and handed it to her. The red foil with the gold printing caused Tracey to pause before she opened it.

"*La Maison Chappelle,*" she read the words aloud. "*Fabrique en Suisse.*"

"Chappelle House," Louise explained quietly. "Have you eaten that brand of chocolate before?"

"Yes, I have," she said with certainty. Her finely arched brows furrowed. "That name, Chappelle..."

"Your father was the U.S. representative for Chappelle House until his death."

Tracey's head flew back and she stared at the other woman. "That's the second time you've mentioned my father."

"Do you remember him at all?"

Tracey shook her head, then rubbed her thumb over the gold embossing on the label. "But I do seem to remember *something* connected with the Chappelle name."

The older woman darted her a shrewd regard. "Maybe that's because it's the most famous name for fine chocolate in the world. Chappelle House is well over a hundred years old. It's a very prestigious company, very established among confection connoisseurs. Go ahead, have a bite."

With a feeling of déjà vu, Tracey undid the wrapper and ate one of the thin squares. "Umm...hazelnut, my favorite. How did you know?"

Louise winked. "I'm psychic. Are you familiar with that word?"

"Yes." Tracey smiled. "So tell me my other favorite kind."

"Hmm... Let me see. White chocolate with little nuts."

Tracey sat back in shock. "You really are psychic."

"No." The other woman shook her head. "A lucky guess. I happen to love nuts, that's all. I'll bring you some next time."

She stood up, considering Tracey for a long moment. "And now I have another surprise for you. There's a lady outside who's anxious to talk to you. But if you don't feel ready to see anyone yet, then just say the word."

Curious, Tracey also got to her feet. "Have I met her before?"

"Yes, about two months ago, but it made no impression on you then. She keeps in constant touch and loves you very much. Here's a picture of her." Louise held out a photograph, which Tracey plucked from her fingers.

At first glance, the picture of the elegant woman staring back meant little to Tracey. But upon closer inspection, the facial features began to be familiar and her throat started to work. "*A-Aunt Rose!*" she finally cried out in recognition.

The doctor beamed. "That's right. Soon you're going to get *all* your memory back. That woman is your Aunt Rose Harris. You were living with her when the accident happened. Do you remember?"

"No. Not a thing. But I know this face."

Eagerly Tracey touched the image that bore a startling resemblance to Tracey's own mother's lovely countenance. Suddenly her father's handsome face flashed in her mind.

"*Daddy!*" she whispered as one tear started, then another, unleashing a myriad of memories from her youth, of a sister and loving parents, of halcyon days of summer surrounded by hillsides of wild narcissus and luscious fruit orchards.

Some of the memories were so poignant and had been dammed up for so long, they came rushing in faster than she could assimilate them. Yet overriding them all was a sudden deep, piercing sadness, too indescribable for words.

Trying to shake it off, she cried, "I want to see Aunt Rose. I *have* to see her," she said, her voice throbbing. "Let me walk out with you," Tracey begged, feeling a sudden compulsion to communicate with the aunt who had taken her and Isabelle in after their parents had died in a plane accident.

"She's in the lounge."

Louise held the door open for her to pass. These days, Tracey could walk normally without a cane and had the run of the floor.

"*Aunt Rose!*"

"*Tracey, darling!*" her aunt called out as they rounded the corner of the hallway.

Tracey flew into her outstretched arms and clung to her, saying her name over and over again.

"Finally you know who I am. I've been waiting ages for you to remember." Rose wept.

"Louise showed me your picture just now and I recognized you."

They both let go of each other long enough to wipe their eyes, then Rose grabbed Tracey's hands. "Four months ago, the doctors said there was no hope, yet here you are alive, amazingly healthy and more beautiful than ever. A miracle has happened."

"At the rate her memory is coming back, she's almost ready to go home," Louise interjected. "Now I'll leave the two of you to your reunion."

"Thank you," Rose murmured to the doctor while Tracey studied her aunt's face, wondering why she hadn't been able to recognize her until today.

The sixty-year-old woman looked a lot like Tracey's mother and sister with her chestnut brown hair. However, where the two older women had blue-green eyes, Isabelle's were brown, like their father's.

As for Tracey, her eyes were a translucent green, darkly lashed, and set in an oval face with high cheekbones and classic features framed by ash blond hair, the odd Saxon throwback her sandy-haired father used to tease her.

"Let's go to your room where we can be private, darling. We have four months of catching up to do."

"Tell me about Isabelle. How is she? How are Bruce and Alex? I just realized I have a sister with a family. Why didn't she come with you?" Tracey asked one question after another as they walked arm in arm down the hall.

Her aunt sobered. "Which question do you want me to answer first?"

They entered her room and shut the door.

"All of them," Tracey cried, so delighted to see her aunt, she felt euphoric. "Come and sit down over here by me," she insisted, patting the couch. The furnishings reminded Tracey more of an elegant hotel suite than a hospital room, a fact her aunt commented on, as well. "Now tell me everything."

"Well..." Rose nervously tucked a loose strand of hair into the back of her chignon. "Your sister would be here, but she's a little under the weather right now."

"Is it serious?"

Rose seemed to ponder her question before saying, "No. Not at all."

"Aunt Rose—I know that look. Something's wrong with Isabelle. Please don't be afraid to tell me. I'm fine and getting stronger every day."

"I can see that, darling, and I thank God for your remarkable recovery. The truth is—" she eyed Tracey uneasily "—Isabelle is expecting another baby and she has dreadful morning sickness."

"Oh, dear. She suffered from that with Alex, too. But how wonderful to be pregnant, to be a mother at all." Her voice ached with longing for things she felt would always elude her, like a family of her own.

In her turmoil, she was scarcely aware of Rose's hands twisting convulsively in her long strand of pearls, or the fact that she'd averted her eyes.

"Is Bruce excited?"

"I—I'm afraid he's too busy thinking of ways to bankrupt them to realize what's happening. I hope he wakes up before it's too late."

Tracey nodded. "So do I." On a burst of energy, she jumped to her feet. "Just as soon as I'm released, let's drive over to Sausalito and surprise them! I can't wait to hold Alex again. While he was having his second birthday party, I was in that coma. To be honest, I can't wait to get out of this place." She cast a guilty glance at her aunt.

"I don't mean to sound ungrateful. Everyone here keeps telling me I'm a living miracle and I believe them. They've been absolutely wonderful to me. But I feel like my whole life has been spent inside these walls. I—I'm starting to get claustrophobia."

"Of course you are. Anyone would feel the same way." Rose got to her feet and put an arm around Tracey's shoulders, commiserating with her. "The doctors only plan to keep you here a little longer."

Tracey sighed. "I wish I could leave with you right now. To be so near the ocean, yet not see or smell anything... Oh, Aunt Rose, I can't wait to go out on the Bay. It will be heaven to sail under the bridge and feel the wind in my face again." When her aunt didn't say anything, Tracey turned to her. "Aunt Rose? Something's the matter. You're acting different...strange..." Tears stung her eyes. "A-am I a freak of nature or something? Did the doctors tell you I'm not quite all there anymore?"

"Oh, no, darling. Anything but."

Suddenly Tracey was enfolded and allowed to cry out her tears against her aunt's soft cashmere sweater that carried the unforgettable scent of roses, her signature for as long as Tracey could remember.

"I thought you would realize that you're in Switzerland, not San Francisco."

Tracey blinked. *Not in San Francisco*?

When Rose's words registered, Tracey pulled away, appalled by the revelation because she should have figured it out long before now.

She shook her head in consternation. "I'm really a mental case, aren't I?"

"Of course you're not!"

Groaning, Tracey clasped her arms to her waist. "No wonder Louise won't let me out of here yet. I'm like a newborn baby who doesn't know anything." Fresh tears spilled down her cheeks. "Maybe I'll never be well enough to leave here."

"Hush, darling. Don't talk that way. You've lived through an ordeal not many humans have ever survived. And don't forget. French comes as easily to you as English because you've been bilingual since you were a little girl."

Tracey moistened her dry lips. "You don't have to make excuses for me."

"*Excuses*? You've been busy healing, getting your memory back. You've done it so fast, you've astounded the entire medical staff here! Of course you're not completely oriented yet. You haven't had time to make a connection with the outside world. But, darling, none of it matters."

"Of course it matters," Tracey lashed out in self-deprecation. "I should have caught on immediately. Look at the ornate furniture in this room. And the food I've been eating! *Escalope de veau* is hardly California's Jack in the Box style, is it? Where am I, exactly?"

"You're in Lausanne."

"*Lausanne*?"

"Yes."

Tracey let out an angry laugh. "The place where they have all the famous clinics for the most serious maladies afflicting mankind. The place where you have to be a wealthy movie star or a Greek shipping tycoon to even begin to afford it.

"Is that where I am, Aunt Rose? In one of those fantastically expensive facilities that has used up all of the inheritance Father left Isabelle and me as well as your modest retirement income?"

Rose walked over to her and cupped the side of her hot cheek with her hand. "You're in a hospital for recovering head injury patients, getting the help you need. That's all that's important."

"Not if *you've* been left with nothing to live on! I couldn't bear that, not after your sacrifice," Tracey agonized. "You could have married again if it hadn't been for us."

"That's not true, Tracey. I didn't want to marry Lawrence. We were just good friends."

Tracey shook her head. "I don't believe that, and I want to see the horrendous bill I've been running up to this point in time. Then I'm going to pack my bags and fly to San Francisco where I'll get an apartment and a job so I can start paying you back."

"That's exactly what you're not going to do," her aunt said in a surprisingly firm tone.

"I know you'd do anything to protect me, Aunt Rose. But I'm a big girl now. My doctor told me I couldn't leave here until I was ready to function in the real world again." She paused for a fortifying breath. "Paying one's own way is part of living in the real world. After four months of being reliant on you, of keeping you separated from Lawrence, it's time I justified my own existence."

"Tracey... I never could bring myself to marry Lawrence, not after what your uncle and I shared. Besides, Lawrence died three months ago of a heart attack."

"Oh, Aunt Rose," Tracey moaned and hugged her again. "I'm so sorry."

"Don't be. He's with his wife now. What's important is *you*."

The note of strain and agitation in her aunt's voice checked Tracey's movements. "You sound so serious. What's wrong?"

"There's nothing wrong. That's why I hate to see you excite yourself needlessly over money. A-all along someone else has been responsible for the bills, so you're not to worry about that."

Someone else?

Since her accident, there were many things Tracey still had to relearn, but no one had to teach her about the soaring of hospital costs in the nineties. Her treatment had to be in the hundreds-of-thousands-of-dollars range by now, if not more.

"Aunt Rose, what person do you know who would have that kind of money, let alone be willing to pay for *my* medical bills?"

"I can answer that," said a deep, velvety male voice directly behind Tracey.

Seized by inexplicable fear, she broke out in a cold sweat, unable to turn around and face whoever it was because she'd heard that voice over and over in her nightmares.

"Julien!" her aunt cried out in alarm, making gestures for him to leave.

Julien Chappelle...

Like a rock thrown at a plate glass mirror, the sound of his name on her aunt's lips made something burst inside Tracey, shattering the shell of her fragile defense system into infinitesimal pieces, leaving her core exposed and bleeding....

She didn't have to turn around and look at him to remember. His jet black hair and eyes, his tall, lean body, those aquiline features so full of character, so incredibly male and breathtaking were indelibly inscribed on her mind and heart forever.

He made every man she'd ever met or dreamed of fade into insignificance beside him. No man could ever be his equal, not in any way. It simply wasn't possible. Tracey loved him more than life itself.

But it was a forbidden love.

Suddenly every atom of her body was filled with that soul-destroying pain she'd lived with for months before the accident. A pain only the coma could camouflage. But even that cocoon of unreality hadn't lasted long. Now the pain was back, more fiery, more unendurable than ever....

"*Dear God...*" she groaned in agony.

That awful sickness welled up in her throat and she barely made it to the bathroom in time.

"Tracey," he murmured anxiously in that low, husky tone she loved so much, having followed her inside the Italian-tiled room to steady her from behind while she retched over and over again.

Don't touch me, she screamed from within when she felt him slide his hands familiarly around her upper arms like he used to do on their honeymoon as a prelude to making love. They couldn't bear to be apart from each other, not even for short periods of time.

Every time he touched her, it was like the first time. But right now she was too violently sick, too weak from the shock of being in his presence again to say a single word.

"If you don't mind, Monsieur Chappelle, I'll take over now," she heard Gerard, one of the nurses, say with an underlying trace of command.

"I do mind," he ground out. "She's my *wife!*"

Tracey almost collapsed from the ring of love and fierce possession in his voice. She couldn't allow this to continue another second.

"*Julien*. Please!" This from Aunt Rose. "We'll wait in the lounge."

Tracey felt the tremor that passed through Julien's powerful body, witness to his tremendous struggle before he finally relinquished his hold of her, leaving her more devastated than ever.

"I'll be back, *mignonne*," he vowed in a hoarse whisper she felt to every tiny hair follicle of her skin.

When she heard their footsteps fade, she slumped heavily against Gerard, who assisted her to walk from the bathroom to her bed.

"Don't let him come back in, Gerard," she begged as he helped her to sit and started taking her vital signs. "He's not my husband anymore. Keep him away from me. Please. I don't want to see him!"

Her relief was exquisite when he said, "Until the doctor says otherwise, no one's going to be allowed in here except the staff. Get ready for bed. Louise is on her way."

"Yes. I need Louise. I need her now!" she cried in panic.

After Gerard left the room, Tracey hurried over to the dresser and changed into a nightgown. Being sick to her stomach had depleted her strength. All she wanted to do was lie down and pray for oblivion.

No sooner had she climbed in bed and drawn the covers over her than Louise strode in, her lab coat flapping. The two women eyed each other as the doctor pulled up a chair next to Tracey and sat down.

"You've had quite a day. You've also made some major breakthroughs that we need to talk about before you go to sleep."

Tracey squirmed to a sitting position, unconsciously drawing the edge of the sheet to her mouth with her hands. "I'll never be able to rest knowing *he's* just down the hall, able to walk in at any time. He's determined to see me." Her voice quaked in fear.

"He's already left the hospital with your aunt. I asked them to leave and watched them drive off."

"Thank heaven." She couldn't have faced him again.

"When he realized that his presence brought on your sick spell, he didn't need anyone to tell him to go. You have to understand that he's spent every night with you for the past three months, trying to soothe you during your nightmares. His devotion has been phenomenal."

Tracey's heart was pierced anew. *Forgive me for doing this to you, Julien, but it's the only way things can be from here on out.*

"Tell me about your husband."

Tracey's fingers locked in a death grip. "He's not my husband."

"Because you don't want him to be?"

The question drove her to explain, "We're divorced."

"He's paying your hospital bills."

Hot tears trickled down her cheeks. "I know. My aunt told me. It's her fault."

"That he's paying the bills?"

"No. That he found out where I was hiding. She's to blame. He broke her down and got the truth out of her b-because she's always thought he was the most wonderful man who ever lived, which of course he is," she said, her voice wobbling precariously.

"I see. So his wealth wouldn't have tempted her to ask for a financial favor?"

"No. Never. My hus—Julien would have insisted on paying for everything. He's always been like that."

"Always? How long were you married?"

"Two months, but our families had been friends for many years before that. The fact is, h-he's the most honorable man alive. His goodness, his decency to people is well known. He's exceptional," she murmured in an aching voice. "That's the problem.

"E-even though we're divorced, I'm afraid he'll always feel a sense of obligation and duty where I'm concerned because that's the way he's made. It would be useless to tell him I want to pay for everything myself now that I'm on my own. H-he wouldn't let me."

"Let me see if I'm understanding you correctly. You think he's the most wonderful man alive and you're not afraid of him. You simply don't want to live with him anymore."

"*Yes!*" She grasped at Louise's summation as if it were a lifeline.

"He's still desperately in love with you."

"I know." Tracey lowered her head. "If you don't mind, I don't want to talk about this anymore. I don't want to be in this place anymore. I'm thankful for everything you've done for me. Obviously I wouldn't be alive without your help. But now I'm well. You told me that yourself just this morning."

"That's true. Physically, you're in amazingly good health."

"I want to go home, Louise. I want to go home tonight!"

Louise lounged back in the chair, her arms folded. "Where is home?"

"San Francisco."

"How will you get there?"

"I have enough cash in my purse to take a taxi to the airport in Geneva. I'll phone my sister collect and have her prepay an airline ticket for me. When I get to San Francisco, she can pick me up at the airport and take me home with her. In a few days, I'll get a job and an apartment, and I'll start making my own way."

"In theory, that all sounds fine. Except that you can't check yourself out of the hospital."

Angry flags of color tinted her cheeks. "What do you mean, *I can't*?"

"Your husband admitted you. He's the only one who can say when you leave."

"But I've already told you. He's not my husband! I divorced him."

"That may be true for you, but he never signed those divorce papers. *Legally, you're still his wife.*"

CHAPTER TWO

TRACEY gasped for breath. "You're *lying*!"

"No." Louise shook her head. "I've never lied to you. I never will. By the time your attorney had served his attorney with papers, you had already been hit by that car and were lying in a coma. According to your Aunt Rose, your husband refused to do anything about your marital status because he was too beside himself with grief."

Tracey's hands flew to her mouth. "Then I'm still Tracey Chappelle?"

"Yes."

No! "I—I can't bear it."

Louise leaned forward, compassion shining from her eyes. "I'm sorry this has come as such a terrible shock to you."

"Why didn't you tell me sooner?" Tracey whispered.

"Because it's best when recovering head injury patients remember the past on their own, when it comes back naturally, when the mind is ready to accept new information.

"So far, that's exactly how your case has progressed. That's why you're in such excellent shape. But tonight your husband changed the rules when he insisted on making his presence known. It was a risk, and now I've had to give you some information you weren't ready for. I'm sorry about that. I didn't want to do it, Tracey. I wanted you to remember on your own, but your husband has been in pain too long. When he saw that you recognized your Aunt Rose, he couldn't hold back any longer."

Tracey dashed away her tears. "How much more is there that I don't know about?"

After a brief pause, "I won't lie to you. There's more, but as your doctor, I don't feel that now is the time to tell you. You've suffered enough shocks for one night."

"So what you're saying is, I'll have to stay in here until *all* of my memory comes back on my own, and even then, I'll still be a prisoner until Julien sees fit to release me?" she cried in despair.

"No. I'm not saying that. You've regained most of your memory, an amazing amount. But there's no way to predict if you're going to have total recall or not. Only time will tell.

"Tracey, speaking as your doctor, I have no problem with your leaving the hospital tomorrow. Naturally I'd like to be able to say good-bye to you knowing that you'd dealt with your recurring nightmares. But your release is not contingent on that. The only thing stopping you from walking out of here now is your husband."

"What if I get an attorney?"

Louise's brows met in concentration. "You could. But do you have the kind of money it would take to hire counsel as good as your husband's?"

Tracey already knew the answer to that question. Her shoulders shook in defeat, and once again she was convulsed. "I need to be alone, Louise."

"All right. I'll come back tomorrow and we'll talk."

A paroxysm of tears wracking Tracey's body made her speech jerky, almost incomprehensible, as she said, "G-give m-e s-some-th-ing t-to s-slee-p, p-plea-se—"

"You no longer need medication. Your demon has finally surfaced. Confront it head-on. Then your dreams won't be disturbed and your sleep will be even more beneficial. Good night."

For the first time since she could remember, Tracey felt violently angry with Louise and kept shouting at her to come back and help her, even after the other woman had turned out the light and shut the door.

"Tracey?"

She jumped at the sound of Gerard's voice. For a fraction of a moment, she'd thought— With the hall light shining behind him, his tall body was a mere silhouette in the doorway of her darkened hospital room, reminding her of—of...

He turned on the light. "Have you changed your mind about dinner?"

"No!" she answered with uncharacteristic rudeness.

"How about a cold fruit drink?"

"No. I need a sleeping pill."

"The doctor didn't write orders for that. Sometimes a little *lait chaud* does the trick."

"No, thanks. I've never liked hot milk."

"Then I'll say good-night. If you need me, press the button."

"I'll never get to sleep!"

"Then turn on the television."

"I hate television. Why can't I go outside? I'll walk till I'm tired. You don't know how caged up I feel."

"Dr. Simoness will be on duty in the morning. When he comes in for his morning rounds, tell him how you feel."

"*I can't wait until tomorrow*! H-has Louise gone?"

"I don't know."

"Will you find out, please? Tell her—tell her I need to talk to her again." Tracey felt as if she was going to jump out of her skin if she didn't get some relief.

"I'll see if I can find her."

A few minutes later, Tracey was still pacing the floor when Louise reentered the room and shut the door.

"Gerard tells me you're more agitated than he's ever seen you before. We both know the reason why, don't we, Tracey?"

Tracey's chin lifted and she stared at her doctor through swollen lids. "Louise..." she began. "I've got to get out of here, out of Switzerland. What am I going to do?"

"I know what I'd do," the older woman murmured quietly, but Tracey heard her.

"*What*?"

"You'd have to be strong."

Tracey bristled. "I am strong."

"Strong enough to tell your husband that you no longer want to live with him?" Her brows arched. "That's what he's waiting for, you know. To see you look him in the eye and tell him to his face that it's over. After all, you *did* tell me he's the most wonderful man alive."

Tracey bit her lip hard. "Yes, I did, because he is."

"Then he deserves that much from you, Tracey. By your own admission, and his, he has never broken his marriage vows, has never done anything to jeopardize the bond between you. *You* were the one who ran away from him without explanation, who never let him know where you were, and then ultimately served him with divorce papers."

"I know," she said in a barely audible voice, crushed by the pain she'd inflicted on Julien.

"*I* happen to believe that he's every bit as wonderful as you say he is. And I firmly believe that if you go to him in complete sincerity, then he'll agree to your release from the hospital, and he'll grant you that divorce.

"He won't like it, of course. How could he? He's madly in love with you. But because his love is so unselfish, he'll put your happiness above his own and you can walk away with your secret still intact."

Tracey's head flew up. "*Secret*?"

"Tracey, I've worked with you far too long not to know when you're holding something back from me. It's all right, you know. Anyone is entitled to his or her own secrets. I suppose the trick will be to keep it from him, but as I said, you'll have to be strong."

Tracey averted her eyes. Louise understood everything, and she was right! *The only way out of here was to face Julien*. The time had come.

Please, God, help me find the strength, the words.

Before she lost her courage she said, "W-would you call him tonight and tell him to come over?"

"I could. But if you're really ready to do this, then the phone call should come from you. If he sees a woman who is in complete control of her faculties, who is able to function like a normal human being again, then you'll be twice as convincing." There was a short silence. "I'm on your side, Tracey."

"I know, and I'll never be able to thank you enough." Tracey reached out and embraced her doctor.

"You've come such a long way. You're almost home. I'll pray for you." Louise gave her a pat, then added, "Gerard will bring a phone in here so you can talk to your husband in complete privacy."

"Thank you, Louise."

"*Bonne chance*."

Good luck. Tracey was going to need much more than that to face Julien. She stood where the older woman left her, watching as Gerard came in with an auxiliary phone and plugged it into the outlet.

For several minutes after he went out, she hovered near the writing desk, trying to gird up her courage.

There was no doubt in her mind that Louise had been honest with her. The only way out of the hospital was through Julien. *Tracey would have to put on the greatest performance of her life.*

Her hand shaking, she picked up the receiver and punched in the château's number, which she knew by heart. Solange answered the phone.

Dear Solange...the housekeeper who'd been with the Chappelles long before Tracey's family had started visiting them two months out of the year for business and pleasure. Tracey had only been nine years old when she'd first started traveling to Switzerland, to Julien's world...

"Ma chère Tracey," Solange cried out the second she recognized the younger woman's voice. After effusive tears that warmed Tracey's heart, Solange told her that after Julien had deposited Rose at the front doors of the château, he'd driven off as if pursued by demons. Did Tracey wish to speak to her aunt?

Tracey couldn't handle a conversation with Rose right now and told Solange she'd call her later. After ringing off, she followed her hunch and punched

in Julien's private number at work. He often went
to his office when something was disturbing him.

She glanced at her watch. It was 10:45 p.m. If
he had driven there, he'd be alone. . . .

After six rings, *"Oui?"* came the terse response.

Suddenly Tracey couldn't talk and tried to
swallow to get some moisture back into her mouth.
Finally she said his name and heard his sharp intake
of breath.

"Mon Dieu—Tracey?"

Her fingers tortured the phone cord. Her heart
was racing so fast she felt slightly sick to her
stomach.

"Y-yes. It's me."

"Do you have any idea how long I've been
waiting for this moment?" His voice shook with
love and need and so many other emotions, she
didn't know how she was going to follow through
with her plan. "It is you, isn't it, *mignonne*? I'm
not hallucinating?"

Hot tears trickled down her cheeks. *No, darling.
You're not hallucinating.*

"No. I—I'm sorry to have been sick in front of
you earlier. Louise said that the shock of remembering sometimes upsets your stomach."

"Does this mea—"

"Julien," she interrupted because she could hear
the joy, the hope in his voice, and wanted to stop
him before things went any further. "We have to
talk."

"I'm on my way."

"No!" she blurted in panic. "N-not tonight."

I can't see you tonight. I thought I could, but I can't! I need the rest of the night to prepare myself.

"After all these months of praying for you to say my name, praying that you'd remember me—you're asking me to *wait*?" he demanded in such a pained voice, she wished she'd never started this.

"I'm sorry. It's just that I'm very tired and was hoping you would come in the morning."

"I can't do that," he groaned. "For months I've watched you lying there, your eyes and mind closed to me," he said in thick tones. "At least when you wake up tomorrow, you'll know who I am and can say my name. I'm coming now, but I swear I won't disturb you if you're asleep. I just want to be in the same room with you. Is that too much to ask, *mon amour*?"

Yes. It's too much to ask. But what choice do I have?

"No. I-it's all right."

"À tout à l'heure, petite."

Oh, dear God, what have I done?

Tracey dropped the receiver on the hook. She'd never get to sleep now, not with him in the room watching her. She couldn't trust him not to try to hold her, kiss her, not when his emotions and feelings were running so high.

Whether she liked it or not, she was going to have to face him in the next little while, which meant she needed to be dressed and ready for him in the public lounge where there were no doors he could close to shut out the world.

Quickly she dashed to the bathroom for a shower. There wasn't a moment to lose. This time of night, the traffic was light. In his Ferrari, it wouldn't take him long to get to the hospital, which she had learned was on the outskirts of Lausanne.

Since he'd always preferred her hair long, she deliberately pulled it back in a chignon like her aunt's, and put on her most tailored blouse and skirt with a conservative navy blazer to look as businesslike as possible.

She would wear no perfume and left off her makeup to de-emphasize her features. It was important that she appear confident and look well enough to leave the hospital, yet draw as little attention to herself as possible.

Wearing her medium leather pumps, she left her room and walked to the nursing station opposite the lounge. "Gerard?"

When he heard his name, he lifted his head from a chart he was reading and stared at her in stunned surprise. "What have you done to yourself? I hardly recognize you."

She could tell that he didn't know what to make of her. That was good. "I'm expecting my husband. I'll just wait here in the lounge."

"Would you like some tea?"

"Maybe when he comes?"

"*Bien sûr.*"

She murmured her thanks and sat down on one of several upholstered chairs placed next to a love seat. On the coffee table were some travel magazines. Desperately needing something to do with her hands, she reached for one and started thumbing through it without seeing the pictures or reading the words.

Whenever she heard footsteps in the hall, her heart would start to pound and she'd look up nervously, only to find a staff member or one of the patients passing by.

"Mignonne?"

A slight gasp escaped her throat when Julien suddenly appeared calling her his darling. He'd made no sound to warn her of his coming. She knew she had to look at him, that she couldn't flinch or turn away. Staying seated, she raised her eyes, bracing herself to take a closer look at him.

There were changes that wounded her heart. Lines that hadn't been there before darkened his aquiline features. His black hair was longer than she remembered his wearing it. He was leaner, harder somehow. His black eyes had a hunted look. But for all that, in a dark gray business suit, the kind he wore to work, his male appeal was more disturbing, more attractive than ever, making her moan inwardly.

She could tell he was waiting for her to get up and run into his arms. In the past, that had always been her way. Julien evoked such love and passion, she could never get enough and could never hide how she felt, even with other people present.

In as steady a voice as she could manage, she said, "It's good to see you, Julien. Sit down. Gerard said he'd bring us some tea as soon as you came."

He remained in place, his body taut, his features wooden. She noticed his hands making fists at his sides. "That's all you have to say to me after twelve months of pure, unadulterated hell?" he asked in an agonized whisper.

"I thought I was being perfectly civil. Today was a day of surprises. Not only did I find out that you were the one responsible for putting me in here, for paying the bills, but I learned that our divorce had never gone through because you never signed the papers."

All the time she was speaking, she watched the blood slowly drain from his face and prayed for this cruelty to end as soon as possible.

"That's why I called you. I want a divorce. It's all there in the papers my attorney sent you. I haven't asked for anything from you. Just my freedom."

His chest rose and fell as if he were fighting for breath.

"*On what grounds?*" His words came out more like a hiss.

This was it. This was the moment she'd been dreading. But when she remembered what had to be done, a great calm came over her.

"I won't lie to you, Julien. You and I both know I have no grounds."

His head reared back as if she'd just struck him because he hadn't expected that kind of bald honesty.

Rising to her feet, she walked over to him and tipped her head to look directly into eyes that were black pools of pain.

Hardening herself against the impact of his suffering, she said, "I love you, Julien. I'll never love anyone else. Never doubt that for a moment. But I found out I don't want to be married. I'd like to go back to San Francisco and get on with my life."

Like a man driven over the edge, his hands shot out and gripped her shoulders, bringing her close to his hard body. "Why?" he demanded with a ferocity that would have defeated her under any other circumstances.

Still keeping eye contact with him, she said, "I wish I could explain it, but I can't. When we returned from our honeymoon, I realized I wanted my freedom back and took the coward's way out by running away."

His fingers tightened on her arms, revealing the depth of his agony.

"It was wrong of me, and I'll always regret the pain I caused you by disappearing. You would never be as cruel to me, which should tell you something about the *real* me. I'm not the woman you want to be married to for the rest of your life." *I can't be*.

His piercing eyes searched her face relentlessly, trying to come to grips with this new reality, trying to find some sign of weakness but finding none.

"I left the way I did because I knew you'd ask me why I wanted a divorce, and I wouldn't be able to give you an answer that would satisfy you."

"You're right," he bit out in fury, shaking her. "After what we shared on our honeymoon, nothing you've said or done since makes any sense."

"That's your answer, Julien. What we had in Tahiti defies description. We experienced something out of the ordinary, something no one can ever take away from us."

Because it happened before the veil was so cruelly torn from my eyes.

"What we shared couldn't ever be duplicated because life isn't like that. Now we're back to reality and I want to go my own way. *Alone.*"

He shook his head in total incredulity. "I don't believe you." In the next breath, his mouth descended, crushing hers, trying to evoke the response that in the past had always been his for the taking because she was so deeply and totally in love with him.

But certain information had changed her world forever, and though the flesh was weak, her soul knew this was wrong, wrong enough that Julien could sense a change in her.

When he finally tore his lips from hers and raised his head, her heart broke all over again to see the mixture of pained confusion and anger coming from the depths of his beautiful eyes. Slowly his hands slid down her arms as if he were still feeling, still testing her for any sign of vulnerability.

Standing her ground, she said, "I understand you're the one who must give permission for me to leave the hospital. I'd like to go in the morning."

He stood absolutely motionless, his ashen countenance adding years to his age. Eventually he said in a lifeless voice, "You haven't recovered all of your memory yet."

"I know. Louise told me I might never get the missing pieces back, but I'm still well enough to be released. It looks like my fate is in y-your hands," she said, her voice faltering for the first time. "After the way I hurt you by running away, you now have the perfect opportunity to hurt me back by refusing the divorce and forcing me to remain in here until I remember everything, which might or might not ever happen."

His body gave a great shudder and his mouth had thinned to a dark line. "You think I'm such a monster that I'd shut you away in here out of some perverted form of revenge?"

"No," she whispered in anguish. "But a lesser man might do it, and with much less reason than you. I hurt you, Julien, when I never wanted to. You didn't deserve it and I wouldn't dream of asking your forgiveness when I know there can be none."

Julien said nothing, only continued to eye her strangely until she started to grow uneasy because she couldn't tell what he was thinking.

"If this has something to do with Jacques, rest assured he'll never be allowed to come near you."

She shook her head. "Jacques has nothing to do with anything."

Jacques, Julien's younger brother, had wanted her long before she'd met Julien, who'd been away studying at Cambridge in England. But once Julien returned to Lausanne and Jacques could sense Tracey's interest in his elder brother, he'd gotten her alone and had tried to force himself on Tracey. Before things went too far, a fiercely angry Julien had intervened, warning his younger brother off for good.

After that night, Julien, ten years her senior, had kept a proprietorial eye on Tracey, picking her up from school every day, giving her a job at his office where she could stay busy and do her homework undisturbed. Tracey, who'd always been intrigued by the enigmatic Julien, fell hopelessly in love with him. The forever kind of love.

An unholy love.

Throughout the long, painful silence, Julien was weighing every word, every nuance of meaning in her denial, trying to find the flaw.

Finally, "I'll sign the release papers tonight on one condition," he grated. She drew in a shaky breath that he couldn't fail to notice. "That you come back to the château to live for one month and give our marriage a chance to work. If at the end of that time you still want the divorce, then I'll agree to it."

Dear God. No!

Julien bit out a strangled epithet. "*Mon Dieu*, your face has gone as white as the walls. I'm not suggesting we sleep in the same bed!"

"I *couldn't*."

"You think I don't know that?" he scathed.

"Then why d—"

"I want *proof* that you'd rather live alone," he cut her off brutally. "You were only a bride in my home for four days before you bolted. Surely after the year of hell you've put me through, you could give me, give us, a thirty-day trial."

Now *her* body was shivering. "But it wouldn't be fair to you, Julien."

"You're in no position to judge what's fair to me," he retorted harshly. "Other components make up a marriage besides conjugal love."

"But if that isn't right, then nothing else works," she said, panicking, sensing that she was losing this battle.

"As you said yourself, those two months in Tahiti speak for the kind of passion we shared. Whatever problem you have, it has nothing to do with the way we communicate in bed. Something much more fundamental is going on here.

"You *owe* me a month's time to explore it. If at the end of that period, you still feel the same way you feel right now, *then* I'll set you free."

Julien had laid down his terms.

Louise had asked Tracey if she was strong enough. It looked like she was going to *have* to be. Julien was fighting for his life.

But then again, *so was she*.

"All right. You can pick me up in the morning after Dr. Simoness has made his rounds. I need to pack and say good-bye to everyone who has been so good to me."

If he was surprised at her capitulation, he didn't show it. "I'll be here at nine."

"Julien . . . I'd like to pay for part of my hospital bill with whatever money Father left me."

"I'm still your husband," he reminded her savagely. "While you're married to me, I intend to be responsible for you. I took a vow to love, cherish and protect you, to keep you in sickness and in health, to bestow my worldly goods on you. *I intend to keep that vow, Tracey.*"

I know you do, darling. I know you do, her heart cried out as he wheeled away from her and disappeared down the corridor. *But it isn't possible*

CHAPTER THREE

To TRACEY, the familiar smell of Lake Geneva seemed even more pronounced in the brisk fall air as Julien maneuvered the Ferrari down the tree-lined drive to the front gates of the hospital grounds.

With that effortless masculine grace she remembered so well, he shifted gears and accelerated onto the main road. His car performed brilliantly, eating up the kilometers with a speed that told Tracey he couldn't whisk her away from the clinic and all its attendant memories of grief and pain fast enough.

Since his arrival at the hospital on the dot of nine to check her out, there'd been an underlying possessiveness in his every word and action that alarmed Tracey because Julien could be a terrifying adversary when provoked. He would fight in ways she hadn't even conceived to break her down, but what he didn't know was that she could *not* be broken down, and he would *not* be successful. The knowledge gave her no joy.

Sitting at an angle so she couldn't see him out of her peripheral vision, she let her hungry eyes take in the quiet elegance of the charming residential streets. As they drove, her ears listened to the myriad of Sunday morning church bells pealing throughout the city. Lausanne had always represented paradise to her. A civilized, gracious paradise in which the exciting man of her teenage dreams had first made his appearance. He was at her side right now. All she had to do was reach out and touch him to feel his warm, solid flesh. But she could never do that again.

She could never think of him in that way again.

When they reached the Gothic cathedral overlooking the city, he unexpectedly headed north away from town. She grew anxious and blurted, "W-we're going the wrong way to the château!"

"I'm taking you to breakfast first."

"Please don't bother. I'm not hungry."

"For the first time in a year, I find that *I* am," he murmured in a voice of unmistakable authority. "I've made arrangements for us to eat at the Chalet Des Enfants. You were always partial to its view of the mountains, and the food."

That was true. Long before their marriage, they would usually end their boat rides or long walks at the quaint little inn high above Lac Léman, where they could see the tips of the French Alps across the mirrorlike lake.

In a gentle, teasing mood, Julien would ply her with the most delicious croissants and honey, followed by steaming cups of sweet cocoa. They'd talk for hours about anything and everything. No time with him was long enough. She never wanted any of it to end.

She still didn't!

Unable to bear this kind of pain much longer, she was on the verge of telling him he would have to eat by himself, that she'd stay in the car, when Louise's warning came back to haunt her.

The only way he'll let you go is to convince him you're fully recovered, that you're physically and emotionally strong enough to handle being on your own.

Thirty days to carry off this charade...

Tracey closed her eyes. This was only day *one*, and already the torture was almost beyond enduring.

The sound of the Ferrari gearing down jerked her from this new waking nightmare and she discovered Julien had pulled into the private drive of the chalet, where he levered himself from the driver's seat to help her. But not before his dark eyes took in her pronounced pallor, causing his lips to twist in a painful grimace that spelled unbearable grief and frustration.

Guilt smote Tracey anew because she and she alone had the power to satisfy his curiosity by telling him the truth. But then another door of pain would open, one so much worse, and Julien would never recover.

She'd had many months to weigh her decision and decided that remaining silent was still the only course to follow. No matter how unacceptable her rejection of him might be right now, in time he would come to accept what happened and rally enough to love again.

Julien had a tremendous capacity to love, and when he finally allowed her to disappear from his life for good, there would be other women to fill the void, women eager to become the next Mrs. Julien Chappelle, women who had the *right* to be his wife and give him the family he longed for. If he never learned the soul-destroying truth from Tracey, he'd be free to pursue a new direction in life.

As for Tracey, there was no possibility of her marrying again. Julien had ruined her for all other men a long time ago. Her only solution was to devote her life to a career that would take her around the world and keep her so busy she wouldn't have time to look back or dwell on forbidden memories.

Frantic to keep her distance from him, she jumped from the car—just out of reach of his hands—and hurried inside the timbered hideaway that had always reminded her more of a dining hall in a monastery than a restaurant.

With a sense of déjà vu, she drew close to the warmth from the grate fire that staved off the chill. On this Sunday morning, she only saw one other couple, but was glad for even that small amount of company.

She seated herself at a nearby table without Julien's help, an action he noted with a distinct frown. Yet nothing marred his striking features, she observed with a pang.

In the shadowy interior, his naturally olive skin took on a darker sheen, as did his hair and brows. The firelight flickered in the blackness of his eyes and emphasized the strong bones of his male beauty.

As he sat down opposite her, his broad shoulders blotted out part of the view from the picture windows. She quickly averted her head to school her instinctive reaction to his masculine appeal. The chemistry between them had always been overpowering, and a year's separation had only increased his potent charisma.

But certain facts had changed the way she was permitted to think of Julien. From now on, whenever she looked at him, it would have to be with the detachment she might feel for a close family friend, nothing more.

No sooner had they sat down than the *patronne* of the inn appeared at their table, greeting Julien like an old friend. He gave their order without consulting Tracey. Certain habits could never be broken, and one of them was the fact that Julien had always taken care of her because he knew her tastes and could anticipate her needs without any words passing their lips.

The incredible harmony between them was still there and always would be, she moaned to herself, clutching her hands together in a death grip beneath the table.

When the owner hurried off to the kitchen, Julien didn't speak right away. Instead, he lounged indolently in the chair and watched Tracey. She moistened her lips in a nervous gesture and began the speech she'd been preparing throughout the endless night at the hospital.

"I—I don't think you can imagine how long and empty my days at the clinic have been."

"They couldn't have been any longer or emptier than mine," he grated in raw pain, giving her a further glimpse into his suffering.

Clearing her throat, she said, "Please don't get me wrong. Everyone was wonderful to me and I'll always be grateful to them, a-and to you. Without your intervention, I might never have made a full recovery."

"Thank God you did," he murmured in thick tones, tearing at her emotions even more.

"But the thing is, I'm not used to such inactivity and the thought of staying at the château with nothing to do for hours on end is anathema to me. If I'm to survive this next month, I'd like a job at your office. I know I can be an asset."

There was a sharp intake of breath before he sat forward in the chair, eyeing her with that sobering intensity she could feel to her bones though she didn't look at him directly.

"Your value to the company has never been in question, but the fact is, I'm taking the month off from work to be home with you. We're going to do everything together, and I can assure you, you won't be bored."

Mingled with that undeniable certainty was an assertive note of determination that said he had no intention of letting her out of his sight, let alone his life.

"*No!*"

Her terrified cry reverberated in the hollow room, briefly drawing the other diners' attention. Julien's dark brows lifted a trifle mockingly. Too late she realized her mistake in letting him see how frightened the prospect of being in his company day and night had made her.

He'd been waiting for her first sign of vulnerability, and she'd just allowed him a glimpse of it.

Summoning every bit of courage within her, she lifted her head and stared straight into his eyes. "Louise told me how you've put your life on hold for the past year because of me. I can't live with that guilt, Julien.

"Please allow me to do something constructive part of each day so that you can deal with your business. Because of me, you've been unable to give your full attention to matters far too long as it is! I'm begging you. Let me make up for that in some small way. After I received my language degree in California, I only worked for your company a short time be-before—"

"Before we were married," he broke in determinedly. "A marriage we both wanted from the first day we met, but I had to wait for you to grow up, so don't insult my intelligence by denying it."

I won't, darling. I won't.

For a moment, she felt dizzy and clung to the edge of the table. "A-all I'm asking is that you let me prove to you that your faith in hiring me in the first place wasn't misguided."

His expression grew remote. He gazed back at her through narrowed lids. "If I never stepped inside my office again, the company would survive. The only thing of importance to me is my marriage. I'll move heaven and earth to make it work."

Another moan escaped. This was so much worse than she would ever have imagined.

Swallowing hard, she said, "I've already told you tha—"

"I know it by heart, Tracey," he broke in coldly. "Thirty days is all I have to convince you that you want to live your life with me and be my wife in the Biblical sense. You gave your word."

"I did, but I had no idea you would put your empire in jeopardy for me when it isn't necessary. We can work together at Chappelle House. It will be like old times." She tried to feign a lightness in her voice, but failed.

"Hardly," he bit out with brutal candor, forcing her to remember the rapture of their honeymoon in Tahiti, a honeymoon she now knew should never have taken place. "Up until Rose informed me of your accident, you've had everything your own way, *mignonne*. Now I'm laying the ground rules." His eyes bored holes into her, making her tremble. "We do this my way, or you go back to the clinic. The choice is yours."

A palpable tension hovered between them. "I couldn't go back there again." *I need to get away from you. Away from your life. Forever.*

A gleam of satisfaction kindled the depths of his eyes. She knew that look and shuddered as he murmured, *"Bien.* Then let's enjoy our food. *D'accord?"*

Thankful that the owner had returned with their order, Tracey made no comment. Instead, she forced herself to eat the large breakfast so that Julien wouldn't attribute her lack of appetite to the fact that she hadn't been totally honest with him.

He knew there was a reason why she didn't want to continue in the marriage, a reason she patently refused to divulge. But being Julien, he couldn't and wouldn't accept what she'd told him. He believed that time would reveal the truth and he'd get his wife back.

Somehow, someway, she'd have to convince him that she'd meant what she'd said, that she didn't want to be married anymore.

Tracey had been making it a matter of prayer. Now that they were together again, she'd have to pray even harder for the strength and inspiration to carry this off.

Judging by the way he reached for another helping of croissants, Julien was obviously pleased at the way things were going. Finishing a second cup of coffee, he eyed her broodingly over the rim. "Whatever the reason that sent you rowing down the lake and out of my life, how did you manage to stay lost so long before making contact with Rose?''

She'd been waiting for that question. If their positions were reversed and he had been the one to have disappeared, she would have been so wild with pain she would have riddled him with a hundred different questions upon finding him again. She wouldn't have been able to rest until she'd obtained the right answers.

Under such precarious circumstances, Tracey couldn't help but admire his forbearance and realized that he deserved an explanation.

''I had enough money to get to London. My intention was to find a good job, but without references I was turned down by everyone except a couple who needed a temporary nanny while their permanent one was in hospital. When she came back to her job, I had no choice but to contact Aunt Rose.''

At that admission, his features became an expressionless mask. He put his coffee cup on the saucer. ''Since you didn't go back to work at Chappelle House in San Francisco, what did you do to fill the hours, aside from hiring an attorney to serve me papers?''

His question pained her all over again. ''I—I don't honestly remember. My last memory is of getting on a plane at Gatwick Airport. Apparently Aunt Rose found some place for me to stay wh-where no one would find me.''

"You mean where *I* couldn't possibly get to you," he interjected bleakly. "Not even your sister knew where you were."

Everything he said compounded her guilt. Tracey put fingers to her forehead where she could feel the beginnings of a headache. "All I know is that Rose told me I was hit by a car while crossing a street, but my mind is totally blank for that portion of my life. It wasn't until yesterday that Louise informed me I was still married, that our divorce hadn't gone through."

Julien assimilated what she said, then rose slowly to his feet. In Tracey's eyes, he looked larger than life as he mercilessly gazed down at her. "If you really thought I would agree to a divorce under the circumstances in which you ran away from me, then you never knew me at all. But we're going to rectify that," he vowed with shocking ferocity, tossing his napkin on the table. "Are you ready to go home?"

Home.

Julien's château could never be home to her now, but she nodded her assent and got up from the table before he reached her. Leaving him to deal with the check, she rushed outside and sucked in deep drafts of the pure autumn air, which was even cooler up on the forested mountainside.

Her sweater dress with its matching blue wool jacket, an outfit she'd purchased in San Francisco several years before, felt good against the elements. She put up the collar of the loose-fitting garment

against her cheeks while she waited for Julien to
appear and unlock the car.

Since coming out of that coma, all her clothes
were too big for her, but Dr. Simoness had promised
her that within three months she'd be back to her
normal weight, provided she ate proper meals and
exercised regularly.

Right now, exercise was exactly what she needed.
It felt so stimulating to be out in the fresh air, she
wanted to run through the woods until she dropped
from exhaustion. But Julien's presence prevented
her from giving in to that impulse.

She didn't dare be alone with him any longer.

"Let's take a walk, shall we?" Julien's low voice
broke in on her tortured thoughts. When he cupped
her elbow in that familiar way, which was always
a prelude to something much more intimate, she
thought she'd lose her mind. But somehow she
managed not to pull away from him.

Floundering for the right response, she said in a
quiet tone, "I thought that was what I wanted, too.
But oddly enough, I feel very tired, probably because I didn't sleep well last night. Dr. Simoness
warned me not to overdo it for the first few days.
If you don't mind, Julien, I'd like to get back to
the château and rest for a little while."

A stillness came over him. She could feel the dichotomy of emotions warring inside his hard, taut
frame.

Just when she thought he might insist on having
his way, his hand dropped, and she thought she

heard a muffled imprecation. It made her realize just how much control he was exercising not to pick her up in his arms and kiss them both into oblivion.

Several times throughout their meal, she'd seen that burning look of desire in his eyes, the look that used to turn her body molten with longing. But that was a lifetime ago when she was innocent of certain knowledge. Now everything was different. *Now that look crucified her.*

By tacit agreement, they moved to the car. Hoping the crunch of leaves beneath their feet camouflaged the sick hammering of her heart, she held herself rigid as he put her inside. She didn't take another breath until he was behind the wheel and had switched on the ignition.

Before he pulled out onto the mountain road, she heard him mutter, "*Mon Dieu.* You've lost every bit of color. Why didn't you tell me you weren't feeling well?"

Beneath his angry demand, she detected an underlying note of anxiety. In the past he'd always been solicitous of her needs, had always put her welfare before his own. That deep concern was in evidence now, even stronger than before, *if* such a thing was possible.

Suddenly it came to her that the situation couldn't be allowed to continue. Thirty more days of this would destroy them completely. Already the past two hours in his company had turned both their lives into disaster.

Since he couldn't know the truth, there was only one thing to do. Before the week was out, she'd find a way to escape and check into a religious retreat where no questions were asked. She knew of such a place high in the Jura Mountains. The nuns welcomed troubled, destitute people who arrived on their doorstep needing to sort out their lives.

Julien would never think to look for her there. All she had to do was bide her time and wait for a day when a delivery truck came from town. She could hitch a ride, or even hide in the back, anything to be long gone from the château, from Julien. But with one fundamental difference.

This time, she'd disappear forever.

"You can forget what you're planning, Tracey." Julien read her mind with stunning accuracy. "We made a bargain and you're sticking to it, even if it means suffering my company twenty-four hours a day. Forget any ideas you've been entertaining about running away. It won't happen again."

Feeling trapped and helpless, she cried, "I need my privacy, Julien."

Those long, lean fingers she could easily imagine around her neck tightened on the steering wheel. "I've already given my word that I won't invade your bed. But be warned, that's as far as my magnanimity extends."

He might as well have sworn an oath.

Immediately Tracey realized her mistake in leaving the clinic. What a fool she'd been to think she was emotionally strong enough to spend even one second in Julien's company when a secret of such devastating proportions was tearing both of them apart.

They'd been too close, shared too much. In time he'd break her down, and once he knew the truth, not only Julien, but both their families, would be destroyed forever.

The only choice left to her was to starve herself until Julien was forced to put her back in the hospital. She'd heard Dr. Simoness, the head of the medical staff at the clinic, explaining to Julien how important it was that Tracey gain weight. Julien might do everything in his power to keep her at the château, but he'd never prevent her from getting medical help if she needed it.

Once she was back at the clinic, she'd stay there until she found a way to escape. Several people on the housekeeping staff had become her friends. She'd work on one of them to help her.

With her mind made up, she was able to relax somewhat for the rest of the drive, and even made a few conversational observations about the beauty of the grounds as they entered his estate.

But she wasn't prepared for the emotional impact of pulling up in front of his home. For a moment, she was taken back to her youth, to that breathtaking time when she'd first caught sight of the fairy-tale-like château. Such a vision had to include a handsome prince, she'd confided to her sister, Isabelle, who was ten on that trip, only a year older than Tracey.

Isabelle agreed, having been raised on the same *Grimm's Fairy Tales*. With a sense of awe and wonder, the two girls followed their parents inside the structure, which was as magnificent and enchanting as Sleeping Beauty's castle, though on a smaller scale, of course. Walking backward half the time, Tracey and her sister gazed in fascination at the paintings and period furniture.

While Henri Chappelle, the tall, attractive, dark blond man with intimidating brown eyes welcomed the girls to Lausanne and introduced them to his wife, Celeste, Tracey saw some photographs on his desk. Within seconds, she fixated on the center one of Julien, and lost her heart completely.

Through bits and pieces of conversation, she learned that he was the eldest out of Jacques and Angelique and was in his first year of university in Paris. As far as she was concerned, Julien Chappelle, with his dark, fascinating looks, was the personification of a prince come to life.

Isabelle noticed his picture at the same time and was as smitten as Tracey. Over the years and the thousands of miles that separated them from Lausanne each time their family returned to the States after their two month stay, the girls continued to weave fantasies about him.

Then came a day after Tracey had turned seventeen when her prince unexpectedly appeared at the château in the flesh.... Tracey groaned aloud at the disturbing memories, afraid they would always haunt her.

Mortified because Julien had probably heard her, she shook her head to clear it. But if he noticed anything, he didn't comment on it. In fact, he seemed curiously detached as he came around her side and helped her from the car. She had the impression he wasn't worried about her escaping his world again.

This time, she didn't flinch when he grasped her elbow to assist her up the steps. She was feeling so shaky, she secretly welcomed his support and was anxious to get settled in.

"Will it be all right if I stay in the same guest room I once used?"

"I'm afraid it's occupied," he told her briefly.

Maybe he had installed Rose in Tracey's old room. Maybe there were business associates of his staying at the château right now. Tracey hoped as much. Anything to divert Julien's attention away from her.

Perhaps like his father, Julien preferred to negotiate the most important contracts and business transactions at home where the atmosphere was congenial, where he could ply his guests with fine food and after-dinner liqueurs.

"For the time being," he continued in a level tone, "you'll be on the third floor, in the room adjoining mine."

Her first instinct was to scream aloud her refusal. But judging by Julien's mood, he wouldn't care if she alerted his guests and entire staff to their precarious situation. In fact, he'd probably welcome it because it would prove that she wasn't as in control as she pretended to be.

The second they stepped through the massive doors, Solange, Julien's plump, redheaded housekeeper, appeared in the vaulted hallway with its tapestried walls and threw her arms around Tracey, warming her heart. The older woman's raisin eyes didn't miss a detail. No doubt she was comparing Tracey to the way she looked a year ago.

"*Grâce à Dieu*," she cried aloud her welcome. "Thank goodness you're home at last, even if you look so fragile, *mon petit choux*. But *n'inquiéte pas*! Cook and I will have you fattened up in no time. Already she has made your favorite *galette au vin* for you."

Pierced by guilt because of what she was planning to do—knowing it would hurt the staff when she refused the meals they would meticulously prepare in her honor—Tracey hurriedly thanked Solange for everything, then turned to Julien to tell him she needed to go to her room.

But he'd already anticipated her comment, and before she could countenance it, he'd swept her into his arms as if she were light as air, and started up the ancient-looking stone staircase.

"Put me down!" she begged in a low voice so Solange couldn't hear, keeping her head averted so their faces wouldn't touch.

"If I do, I have the feeling your legs will collapse beneath you. Relax, *mignonne*. You're home now and I'm going to take care of you, so don't try to fight me or you'll expend the little strength you have left.''

He was right. Her body felt like mush.

To counteract the feelings such intimacy aroused—memories of his carrying her up the stairs almost exactly this way upon their return from Tahiti, except that their mouths had been fused in passion—Tracey's only weapon was to slump against his chest and pretend to fall into an exhausted sleep.

In truth, it wasn't difficult to do. Since the night before, when Julien's deep, distinctive voice had broken through the barrier to bring her back to stark reality, she'd been so emotionally drained, she craved her bed.

Once they'd entered the elegant suite adjoining his, he laid her down on smooth, silk sheets.

"All I want you to do is sleep, *petite*," he murmured, his lips brushing her forehead with a tenderness that was almost her undoing.

Except for the feel of his hands as they removed her jacket and shoes, she remembered nothing else but the cool of the pillow against her hot cheek and the delicious warmth of the covers Julien drew over her inert body.

CHAPTER FOUR

WHEN next Tracey came awake, the angle of the sun's rays through the mullioned windows alerted her that she'd slept hours. Her watch said 4:36.

Shocked to have been asleep so long, and even more shocked not to find Julien sitting in the love seat guarding her, she threw back the covers of the canopied bed and slid off the mattress, noticing that her bags had been brought up and her things put away while she was unaware.

After padding over the oriental rug into the en suite bathroom, she took a quick shower, then rummaged in the seventeenth century armoire for a pair of jeans and a blouse, her uniform at the clinic once she'd been able to start dressing herself.

Using a navy chiffon scarf to tie back her ash blond hair, which was longer than shoulder length by now, she slipped into loafers and left the room to find Rose. No doubt her aunt occupied one of the rooms on the second floor since the Chappelles reserved the third floor for members of their immediate family.

Tracey had a lot of questions only her aunt could answer. She particularly wanted to know why her mother's sister had felt such an abiding loyalty to Julien that she'd overridden Tracey's wishes, landing her in the untenable situation she found herself in now.

Though she hadn't been inside Julien's home for a year, she knew it by heart, having explored its architectural wonders many times over with Julien's brother and sister. Every corridor running past the various rooms of the spacious château led to the central staircase that wound to the common rooms of the ground floor.

She could make her way blindfolded to the second floor and hurried down the stairs to join Rose, who was probably having tea in her room, her habit this time of day.

But when she heard a baby crying, her steps slowed, and she looked all around, wondering which room housed the sound, trying to imagine who of Julien's acquaintances would be staying at the château with an infant.

It didn't sound like a newborn, but its cry was far too young to be her nephew, Alex. In any event, Julien would have told her if Isabelle and Bruce had come.

To Tracey's knowledge his sister, Angelique, hadn't had a baby yet, so it couldn't be her child unless something had happened in the past year Tracey knew nothing about.

Puzzled, she made her way down the corridor toward the room where she could hear the baby's vigorous voice building to a crescendo. Then came a woman's voice, speaking French in cajoling tones, attempting to hush the child's tears to no avail.

Driven by an instinct she didn't understand or question, Tracey knocked gently on the door that led to Isabelle's old room and was told by an unfamiliar female voice to enter.

Obeying the woman's bidding, Tracey turned the knob, but the sight that greeted her eyes sent her into shock. No longer a guest room, it had been completely transformed into a nursery whose colors reminded her of sunshine.

What was going on here?

What did it mean?

Whose baby was so important that Julien would transform a room of the château into a nursery with every convenience imaginable?

The fortyish-looking stranger, dressed like one of the staff at the clinic, held a squirming baby girl of five or six months against her shoulder. She greeted Tracey cordially enough, but was too occupied with her charge to engage her in conversation.

In a total daze, Tracey swung her gaze to the jet black curls framing a perfectly oval face. Her rounded cheeks were wet and flushed from her crying spell. To Tracey's mind, the baby was the most adorable little thing she'd ever laid eyes on in her life.

She wore a tiny white undershirt and a disposable diaper, displaying sturdy limbs and the kind of cuddly body Tracey loved to squeeze.

Whether the baby had just awakened from a nap, or was refusing to be put down for one, it appeared she wouldn't be comforted.

Obeying blind impulse, Tracey crossed the expanse to get a closer look. But what she saw sent a stabbing pain to her heart.

The dark, finely arched brows that were wrinkled in a frown, the set of the firm little chin wobbling from repeated outbursts, looked increasingly familiar.

As she studied the baby's olive complexion—the shape of the long fingers with their half-moon nails curled into fists of frustration—Tracey was put in mind of the man she loved beyond description.

Julien.

Tracey gasped.

Like pure revelation, she knew this was *Julien's* child. Genes didn't lie. No one but his own flesh and blood would be given such a place of honor in the family home and showered with every worldly possession.

This was his love child.

Obviously he'd turned to another woman after Tracey had disappeared. *Who*? Someone Tracey knew?

Again, stabbing pain tore her to pieces, this time from jealousy, an emotion she'd never had any reason to experience until now.

What was he doing fighting the divorce when there was a woman out there who loved him enough to bear his child and let him raise it as a Chappelle?

Clutching at the nearest support that happened to be the crib, she wondered what kind of insanity drove him to force Tracey to live with him for the next month when it was perfectly obvious he had another woman just waiting in the wings.

But she already knew the answer to that question. Julien was an honorable man and brutally honest. One who, when he discovered that Tracey had awakened from the coma, would give her this last chance to change her mind about remaining his wife before he signed those divorce papers.

Unable to look at the child who should have been, could have been theirs if certain knowledge hadn't come to light, she wheeled around in despair and raced for the door.

Since their own love was forbidden, maybe in time she'd thank providence that he'd been able to turn to another woman for comfort and now had a child of his own to love.

But right now she was in too much agony to bear it and fled from the room, only to career into Julien standing at the threshold with an enigmatic expression darkening his arresting features.

He put out his hands to steady her, but she as quickly backed away from him, unable to bear his touch when it still burned her skin with its fire.

"You've been busy while I was gone," she said in a ragged whisper, using English so that hopefully the nanny wouldn't be able to understand them. She didn't want to sound accusing. She didn't have the right, but she knew she sounded like an insanely jealous woman who'd just been confronted with the naked truth of her husband's perfidy.

"You could say that," he drawled in kind, not acting the least bit uncomfortable or guilty. While she stood there grappling with the indisputable proof of his extramarital affair, he switched to French and asked the woman named Clair to bring him the baby before she went on break.

Clair looked relieved as she placed the howling infant in his arms and disappeared out the door.

The baby soon quieted down and nestled against Julien's shoulder as if to rest against that treasured spot and be loved by her father was what she'd been waiting for all the while.

The light in Julien's eyes left Tracey in no doubt that he adored his little girl. Love was evident in the way his hand roamed over her pliant back, the way his lips grazed her dark curls and neck with kisses until she started to croon in response.

Unable to repress her emotions, Tracey blurted, "Who is she, Julien?"

His black eyes searched hers for an overly long moment. "Her name is Valentine," he said in a low, husky voice. "She was born on the fourteenth of February."

A muffled cry escaped Tracey's throat. "I don't mean the baby. I mean her mother."

After a tension-filled silence, "Who do you think she is?"

His comment brought her up short. "I have no idea," she replied, her voice shaking.

For a split second, she saw a glint of pain in those dark recesses before they became shuttered and he said, "She's the most beautiful woman alive, the only woman I'll ever love."

Tracey lowered her head, cut to the quick by his cruelty. Why in heaven's name would he want to hang on to her, Tracey, when he had just admitted his love for this ravishing creature who'd borne him a daughter?

Unable to stop her mind from wandering, Tracey's imagination conjured up pictures of several women he knew socially and at the office. Too many of them classified as great beauties. But which one had he turned to in his need?

"Take a closer look at Valentine, especially her green eyes and rosebud mouth, then you'll recognize her mother."

Tracey blinked in confusion. *Green eyes? Rosebud mouth*?

But according to Julien, those were Tracey's own characteristics....

Her head flew back and she stared at him, uncomprehending.

His expression grew bleak. "When Louise showed you a picture of Rose, you finally recognized your aunt. I was praying that when you saw Valentine, you would realize she's *our* daughter, Tracey. Yours and mine."

"*Our* baby?" she half groaned the question and staggered on her feet so that he was forced to help her to a chair.

"*Oui, mignonne*. Ours and no one else's. Valentine is six months old. If you work out the time frame, she had to have been conceived on our honeymoon."

"B-but that's im-impossible," she whispered in shock.

"Nevertheless, the impossible happened," he insisted quietly. "Feel free to call Hillview Hospital in San Francisco. She was delivered by Dr. Benjamin Learned. Examine her closely and you'll see yourself in her smile, in her translucent eyes, which are identical to yours."

He got down on his haunches and placed the baby in her arms, still allowing Valentine's fingers to cling to one of his so she wouldn't cry.

Though Tracey shook her head in disbelief, she felt compelled to obey his suggestion. With fear and trembling, she took a long, hard look at the beautiful baby cradled in her lap. A miracle of creation.

Slowly one sob, then another, shook her body as she recognized various family traits that could only belong to the Marshes and the Chappelles, branding Valentine *her* child. And Julien's . . .

"No!" she cried out as the ramifications of what this meant hit her with full force. "No . . ." she whispered in agony, needing to get out of the room.

Her tormented state communicated itself to Valentine, who didn't like being relinquished to her father so quickly and broke into tears immediately, clutching at Julien's neck with all her force.

"Tracey—*Mon Dieu*—come back here!" Julien called in an anxious voice. But she flew out the door and within seconds reached the safety of her own bathroom on the third floor, where she could turn the lock and examine herself in a mirror.

The accident that had put her in a coma had caused several lacerations on her arms and legs, so she hadn't given any thought to the scars below her navel.

"Good heavens!" she cried to herself when saw the fading pink lines that had been made by a doctor's scalpel and were still healing.

She had to have delivered before her accident!

But how could she have given birth to Valentine and not have known it, not remembered it? *How was that possible*?

At the clinic, when Louise had told her there was still more of her past to recall—that it would be best if she remembered it on her own—Tracey had had no idea. No idea at all...

"Tracey?" Julien called to her from the bedroom. The next thing she knew he was knocking on the door. "Tracey... I know this has come as a tremendous shock to you. Let me in. We have to talk."

No wonder Julien had made that bargain with her.

He knew her child was waiting for her back at the château. A child who should never have been born.

A child who most likely would have defects and problems she couldn't bear to think about.

Tears ravaged her cheeks. She buried her face in a towel to stifle the sound. "Go away, Julien," she begged, sobbing hysterically.

"I can't, *mon amour.* Now that you've met Valentine, you need to know everything so there won't be any more shocks."

She lifted her head. "W-what do you mean, more? How could there be a-any more?"

"Open the door and find out."

Traumatized by the revelation that she and Julien had brought a child into the world, Tracey couldn't bring herself to turn the lock. She slumped against the door in an effort to stay upright.

That's when her ears picked up the unmistakable sound of Valentine's voice. But she thought she heard the noise of another baby, as well. Maybe she was hallucinating, so she listened more intently as Julien spoke in gentle, soothing tones, his tenderness reaching her soul.

"We're not going to go away until you come out, Tracey. Open the door. Raoul and Jules have been wanting to say hello to their *maman* for a very long time."

Jules? Raoul?

The names reverberated in her head and suddenly another dam broke, releasing the last torrent of suppressed memories: the sounds of her babies all crying at once as she entered the hospital's preemie unit. Three babies, born a month early.

Babies she'd named without Julien's knowledge, thinking he would never know, never find out. Babies who might never be normal.

"Tracey!"

Under ordinary circumstances, the alarm in Julien's voice would have made her reach out to release the lock. But for the life of her, she couldn't move because another memory had intruded on her consciousness, paralyzing her.

Like a flash of lightning that illuminated everything, she had total recall. Her flight from England, the shocking news that she was expecting triplets, her months of seclusion in the California summer home of a friend of Rose's, the complicated delivery of her three children and the aftermath, the days and nights she'd spent holding them, feeding them, memorizing each perfect feature and the differences in personality.

She remembered many long hours in the darkness of night when she'd kept an anxious vigil in the preemie nursery, loving them, feeding them, changing their diapers, planning how she was going to take care of them and raise them without Julien's help.

My babies, she groaned as an overwhelming wave of love and longing for them swept through her. *Five months* she'd been separated from her precious children—five months that someone else had been a mother to them.

But they hadn't gone without love. Julien had been there for them from the beginning, had bonded with them, showering them with the kind of attention only he, their marvelous father, could provide, while she—

The taxi!

She remembered the day she was set to take the babies home from the hospital, remembered her anger and frustration against Rose before getting out of the car. They'd been arguing violently because Rose was on Julien's side and didn't approve of Tracey asking him for a divorce without telling him about his children.

She remembered slamming the car door and running into the path of an orange taxi unexpectedly coming at her from the right. Then everything went black.

The same kind of blackness enveloping her now...

"Louise!"

"Bonjour, Tracey."

When Tracey realized it wasn't Julien, she sat up higher against the pillows, trying to pull herself together. First Dr. Simoness, now Louise.

When Tracey had refused to see or talk to Julien after the head of the clinic had examined Tracey last evening, Julien must have sent for Louise, knowing how close Tracey felt to her.

The older woman came into the bedroom and shut the door. Without asking Tracey's permission, she pulled one of the matching damask chairs next to the bed and sat down.

"W-what are you doing here?" Though Tracey already knew the answer, she was so frantic she'd said the first thing to enter her head.

"Locking the bathroom door gave your husband quite a fright," the doctor replied in mild chastisement. "As I understand it, he had to break it down to get to you, fearing your faint might have sent you into another coma."

Tracey shivered as a fresh attack of pain and remorse almost incapacitated her.

"When Dr. Simoness arrived at the château in response to his phone call around dinnertime, he said your husband was in as bad a mental state as you are."

Lowering her head to avoid Louise's probing gaze, Tracey's anxiety over Julien finally forced her to ask, "I-is he all right now?"

"What do you think?"

A dreadful silence prevailed before she blurted, "I can't stay here any longer, Louise! Julien let me out of the clinic on the condition that I live under the same roof with him for thirty days, and if at the end of that time I still wanted a divorce, then he'd give it to me. I thought I could do it, but—"

"But you never wanted children because you're not the marrying type, and now that you've found out you're the mother of triplets, you're repulsed by the idea.''

"*No!*" Tracey cried in horror at Louise's misconception of the situation.

Instead of looking surprised, her doctor actually seemed gratified by Tracey's outburst. Too late it dawned on her that the other woman had tricked her into revealing her true feelings.

"That's what your husband is beginning to believe, you know. He tells me you've refused to look at your sons, even to acknowledge them.''

Louise knew exactly what to say to reach Tracey, who threw back the covers and got out of bed. The view of the lake was particularly beautiful from her window, but all she could see was Julien's tormented expression when she'd come out of her faint. His agony, coupled with her own, had finally brought her to the breaking point.

Wiping the moisture from her cheeks, she wheeled around to face Louise.

"I'm *a-afraid* to look at them,'' she admitted shakily, remembering the strong Chappelle characteristics she saw in Valentine.

"Because they're replicas of your husband and you don't want to live with him anymore?''

"*No!*" Her denial resounded in the room. Louise said nothing, but her eyes invited Tracey to unburden herself. After another tension-fraught pause, Tracey found herself saying, "I—I can't bear to look at them—f-for fear I'll see Julien's *father* in their features.''

"But that would only be natural, wouldn't it, seeing he's the grandfather?"

"No! You don't understand." Tracey groaned. "Henri Chappelle is *my* father, too."

"*Ahh...*"

There was a wealth of understanding in that one word. Tracey could sense Louise studying her through new eyes, her mind obviously computing this latest revelation with all its damning ramifications.

"Tell me something, Tracey. Was Henri Chappelle a tall man with an imposing countenance and dark, piercing eyes?"

Tracey's head whipped around. "Yes. He's *exactly* like that. How did you know? Have you seen a picture of him? Do my sons resemble him that much?" she asked, her voice throbbing in agony.

"I've never seen your children, but I do have a picture of your father-in-law in my possession. It's the one you drew for me day before yesterday," she said softly.

"*What*?"

Louise nodded. "That wasn't an animal you sketched. It was a man in the shape of a bird of prey, an eagle to be exact. You've just provided me the missing piece of the puzzle. *He* was the cause of your terrible nightmares."

Tears poured down Tracey's cheeks.

"The second I saw the drawing, I knew it couldn't be your husband, and it certainly wasn't your father, because your aunt had already shown me pictures of your family."

"Except that Daddy's not my daddy," Tracey whispered in a stricken tone.

Louise's hands went to the pockets of her suit jacket. "I presume it was Henri Chappelle himself who told you his terrible secret after you and your husband returned from your honeymoon."

"Yes."

"That explains your precipitous flight."

"Yes."

"Deathbed repentance on his part?"

Tracey nodded as more tears dripped down her face. "He could barely get the words out about his affair with Mother before Monseigneur Louvel came in to perform the last rites."

On her feet now, Louise approached Tracey. "*Ma chère*...I can't tell you how sorry I am. I wish there were some magic words to make the pain stop."

"I wish I were dead."

"I can understand why you would feel that way," Louise commiserated. "After living as man and wife, to be asked to treat your beloved Julien like a brother is asking *too* much.

"Now we know why your mind suppressed all memory of your pregnancy and delivery for such a long time. It makes perfect sense. That, and the guilt, because you're incapable of viewing Julien in any other light than your lover."

"Yes." Tracey broke down sobbing and felt the older woman's arms go around her. Louise understood everything.

"But no matter how much pain you're in, you have two handsome sons and a beautiful daughter to consider. Three infants who need their mother. You must live for *them*, Tracey."

Tracey's shoulders shook and it took a few minutes to recover her composure before she moved out of Louise's arms. "I know."

"Naturally you're afraid that because you and your husband are half brother and sister, your children will have abnormalities, which might or might not be the case. Check with the pediatrician right away and put your fears to rest."

"I—I'd already planned to do that this morning."

"Good for you. But please remember. Whatever you learn and have to deal with, it will be better than the agony you've suffered since returning from your honeymoon."

"I—I came to that conclusion last night," Tracey concurred in a piteous voice.

"There's something else." Louise eyed her shrewdly. "You're going to have to break the silence and tell your husband, Tracey."

CHAPTER FIVE

"*I COULDN'T possibly*!" Tracey cried out, shaking her head.

"Every day is a new nightmare for him," the doctor reasoned. "He doesn't deserve it."

"But the truth will destroy him. It will change the way he feels about his entire world! Nothing will ever be the same for him again," she retorted despairingly.

"Nothing has been the same for him since you disappeared. Don't you know that *you* are his entire world, you and the children?"

"Please don't say that," Tracey appealed to her. "People get divorced every day and survive it."

"Not people who love as profoundly as you and your husband have loved each other."

Tracey couldn't stand to listen to any more. "In time he'll find someone else to love and it won't be forbidden."

"He has the right to know, Tracey, and you don't have the right to keep it from him. Look at the damage done because your mother and Henri Chappelle lived all these years holding on to their guilty secret."

Tracey felt like she was in some sort of trance, hardly aware of speaking her thoughts aloud. "It's no wonder I wasn't invited back to the château."

"Tell me about that portion of your life. We could never talk about it before because of your memory loss."

Tracey needed little encouragement. Now that Louise knew the truth, it was easy to fill in the missing portions of her life for her.

" ... so I guess when Mother and Henri could see what was happening between Julien and me, they separated us and the family visits ended for good. Only Isabelle was allowed to stay with Angelique for a few weeks at a time out of the year, while I—" her voice caught "—was never invited back." Her heart ached with resurging sadness. "I wonder if Daddy knew."

"If he did, it obviously never changed the way he felt about you. Not only that, he must have loved your mother enough to forgive her," Louise commented at last. "Otherwise it doesn't make sense that he remained her husband and stayed with Chappelle House until his death."

Tracey passed a trembling hand over her eyes. "I'm sure you're right. When I think about it, I never really believed that Celeste's failing health was the reason our family had to remain in San Francisco. She'd always been fragile, so it didn't make any sense to me that she suddenly couldn't cope with guests. Henri always had plenty of staff to see to her needs.

"I never did come right out and ask Julien about it, but I'm positive he didn't believe it, either. He probably thought the permanent separation had something to do with Jacques and me. That must be why he insisted on our marriage taking place in private without either family's knowledge. I doubt he told anyone about our wedding plans when he left Switzerland on business."

Louise cocked her head. "So now it's time for the whole truth to come out. If you keep this from your husband, you'll not only hurt him irreparably, but you'll be compounding your parents' sin in a way that could one day rebound on the heads of your children."

Her words terrified Tracey.

"Louise, this doesn't affect just Julien and me. There's our brothers and sisters to consider. News of such a scandalous nature would rock close family members and friends on both sides of the Atlantic.

"Right now, I'm the only one who knows the truth except for you. I—I can't risk it." She bit her lower lip so hard it bled. "Julien will be in pain for a while, but he'll eventually get over it and carry on with his life."

Louise shook her head. "You know that's not true. He won't get over it, Tracey. I watched him at your bedside every night for months, attempting to comfort you during your nightmares, willing you to recover. His love for you transcends everything else."

She pressed Tracey's arm gently. "If you truly love him, you'll tell him everything. Both sets of parents are dead now, so they can't hurt or be hurt anymore. Scandals die, you know. But the truth is the only way to free your husband. Then, and only then, will he be able to find someone else to love, *if* that is his choice. Don't you see that otherwise you'll be condemning him to a prison he didn't make?"

Tracey stiffened. "If Henri had thought Julien could handle it, he would have told him the truth instead of me."

"Nonsense," Louise came back firmly. "I've learned enough from what you've just told me to know that Henri Chappelle went selfishly to his grave, content that his elder son still worshiped him.

"It was easy enough to rid his conscience with you since your mother had already passed away and he no longer required her permission to act. He also knew your character well enough to count on your loyalty, knowing you'd keep his secret rather than destroy the family.

"*Think about it*! The second he slipped from life, you disappeared on cue. Don't you understand that he manipulated you and is still continuing to do so?"

Twisting her hands together, Tracey blurted, "I can't do it, Louise. Julien and his father were very close. I couldn't bear to damage that. Promise me you'll never tell a living soul."

"I made that promise when I became a doctor, Tracey. Whatever you've told me remains confidential, but I'm warning you. You'll keep this secret to your own peril." Heaving a sigh, she said, "I'm going to leave now. You know where to find me if you wish to talk about it further. Just remember one thing. I'm on your side. Always on your side."

"Thank you, Louise."

After following the older woman to the door, Tracey hurried into the shower, her mind racing ahead.

Maybe the pediatrician would see her before the day was out. She needed to be dressed and ready in case she was told to come in at her earliest convenience.

There had to be tests Tracey could arrange to determine if there'd been any genetic damage to the babies.

Julien wouldn't think it strange that she wanted to see the children's doctor. Any woman who truly loved her children and had been separated from them this long would do as much. In fact, he would be more than pleased that she was taking so much interest in their welfare. No doubt he would view her actions as a positive sign that she was coming around to the idea of being a mother. *And a wife. Darling Julien. If only you knew . . .*

Hurriedly she put on the same outfit she'd worn home from the hospital, then rushed out of the room. But her flight was short-lived because Julien came striding toward her with purpose in every step.

Quickly she averted her eyes, but not soon enough to blot out the devastatingly attractive picture he made. In a navy polo shirt and khaki trousers that molded his powerful body, his casual attire reminded her of their honeymoon.

Julien hadn't taken any formal clothes to Tahiti. The two of them were much like children of the sea, playing and loving anywhere they felt like it, often without the benefit of clothes.

On the rare occasion when they went to the nearby village for dinner, they dressed informally, with her wearing a native wraparound he'd bought for her, and Julien sporting the kind of outfit he was wearing now.

Those memories went soul deep. *How was she ever going to erase them?*

"Louise's visit must have done you some good. Your color is back." His low, velvety voice broke in on the heavy tension between them.

"Yes," she responded, her breathing shallow. "W-we've been talking about the babies."

"Tracey," he said on a ragged whisper, "I should have told you about the children last night before I left the clinic. But because you didn't recognize me until I spoke to you, I assumed the same miracle might happen again when you heard our children crying or saw them in my arms."

"I-it did happen. Your plan worked. There are no more memory gaps. I remember everything, even the color of the taxi that hit me."

At the mention of the accident, his face blanched. "But at what cost?" he bit out in self-denigration.

"It was better this way, Julien. Your instincts are rarely wrong. I'm glad to know the whole truth. That's why I was coming to find you, to tell you that I'm all right now. You don't need to worry about my having a relapse or any such thing."

He stood with his strong legs slightly apart, those dark winged brows forming a skeptical frown as he rubbed the back of his neck in an unconscious gesture she'd seen before. It meant that he patently didn't believe her.

"Actually, I feel good enough to visit the children's doctor," she assured him. "Today, if possible."

He blinked, obviously puzzled. "Why? If you're worried about them, you don't need to be. I can promise you they're in perfect health."

His comment was reassuring enough on the surface, but she wanted to know a great deal more than that.

One black brow dipped in concern. "*Mignonne*, if you're suffering over Raoul, then don't. It's true that before the accident, he was the one who had the most difficulty breathing on his own, but that problem cleared up after a couple of weeks."

"Thank heavens for that," she murmured in heartfelt gratitude. "Look, Julien. I believe you." Her hands twisted together nervously. "But it's just that I've missed so much of the past five months, I want to know all there is to know about their medical histories and development before I get reacquainted with my precious babies.''

Searching for any plausible excuse, she continued, ''I—I want to see their growth charts and what they've eaten and liked and disliked. You know.'' Tears welled in her eyes. ''All the little things a mother normally knows about her children.''

Whatever he'd been expecting her to say, her words caught him off guard. Judging by the way the hard muscles of his body appeared to relax, she knew she'd pleased him.

''Having been deprived of them this long, naturally you have questions,'' he concurred with a gentleness that was too piercingly sweet. ''I'll arrange it with Dr. Chappuis right now, *mignonne*.''

Stop calling me that, her heart cried out. Somehow, someway, she was going to have to school herself not to react every time he used one of his special endearments for her. ''I realize he probably has a full schedule so—''

''If he's not at the hospital, I'll make certain he sees us this morning,'' Julien murmured, making it sound like an avowal.

Not *us*, she moaned inwardly. But that was another thing she was going to have to get used to. Julien meant what he said when he told her they would be doing everything together for the next month.

''Where are the children now?''

"Out for a walk in their prams. It's a beautiful autumn day." What he didn't say with words, his eyes were telling her. That it was the kind of glorious morning the two of them used to relish.

Julien, don't get your hopes up. Please, darling.

"Well—" she cleared her throat "—if you don't mind calling the doctor, I'll run to the kitchen for some breakfast."

Without waiting for a response, she hurried down the corridor to the stairs, praying Julien wouldn't follow her.

To her intense relief, he wasn't behind her as she entered the kitchen and interrupted Solange, who was delighted to see her and began plying her with hot chocolate and melt-in-your-mouth brioches dripping with butter and conserves.

Under the circumstances, the idea of starving herself to get away from her husband was not only absurd, but criminal. Her babies needed her. The last thing she wanted was another separation from them because of poor health she'd purposely brought on.

If anything, remembering that she had three children gave her the impetus to put on the weight she'd lost as quickly as possible so she could take care of them without help.

Of course, Julien couldn't have managed without full-time nannies, but now that she was back, things had to change. She didn't want anyone else raising her babies. If Julien was demanding that she stay with him for a month, then she could make demands, too.

Her first request would be to let the nannies go. Julien said the children were in perfect health. Certainly if necessity made it difficult for Tracey to cope on her own, there were enough maids employed at the château to lend an occasional hand.

Not only did Tracey want her babies to herself, she needed to stay so busy that it would keep Julien at a distance until the thirty days were up. Beyond that, she could scarcely think. Since Julien would never let his children go, maybe she could get an apartment near the château so that they could share them on a daily basis.

She would watch over them during the day, and Julien could take care of them after he left his office, if that was what he wanted. Sort of a joint custody situation that would give him the space he needed to build a new life with someone else. It could work. *She'd make it work*.

Gone were her plans of a career and travel. She was a mother now, something she'd always wanted to be. There was no question in her mind that Julien would provide for her so that she could give their children all the love in her.

It would be her mission to raise them. To bathe and cuddle them, to play with them and read them her favorite stories. To teach them how to talk and sing and pray, how to love and give love, how to be perfect little ladies and gentlemen their daddy would be proud of.

She couldn't wait to immerse them with love. What better outlet to sublimate her love for Julien than by devoting her life to their children.

"Tracey?"

Her head swerved in Julien's direction. She'd been so deep in thought, she hadn't heard him enter the kitchen.

"Dr. Chappuis's nurse said he's still at the hospital doing rounds, but he's expected back shortly. We're to come as soon as we can get there and she'll fit us in."

Frightened, yet relieved that she'd have answers shortly, Tracey finished swallowing the last of her roll before she said, "Thank you for arranging it, Julien. Give me a minute to run upstairs and get my purse."

"I brought it down with me to save you a trip."

Julien thought of everything and was always five steps ahead of her. Not only that, he'd accomplished a minor miracle. Most pediatricians' offices were so overbooked with sick children, getting in to see the doctor on an unscheduled visit was close to impossible.

When he handed her the tan leather purse she'd brought from the hospital, the touch of his fingers felt like the lick of brush fire against her skin. She quickly pulled away.

His sudden grimace let her know he was aware of her reaction, and his terse "Shall we go?" didn't bode well for the rest of the day as she thanked

Solange and followed him out to the Ferrari parked at the rear of the château.

The second she stepped into the warm sunshine, she was reminded of other such beautiful fall mornings when the mist on the lake had already dissipated. With a pang of longing, she remembered the two of them stealing away from the house so they could enjoy a few hours alone together, whether it be on a boat ride to visit a castle, or a picnic in the mountains, surrounded by fields of wild narcissus.

Unlike now, however, there had been this incredible harmony between them and an almost sick sense of excitement on her part because she was going to have him all to herself.

Once alone, she'd do everything in her power to get him to kiss her, but he always stayed in control, never giving in to the passion she felt sure he was capable of.

He never showed the sensual side of his nature until he unexpectedly attended her graduation from college. That night, he kissed her for the first time. A kiss that went on and on and transformed her world forever. When he finally released her, he told her they were getting married the next time he came to San Francisco, but she was to tell no one their plans.

She'd been so happy then. *So happy* . . .

"Tracey?"

The sound of her name brought her back to the present. "Yes?" she whispered guiltily.

"Valentine has your exact profile. She's perfect. Do you have any idea how incredible it is to look at her and see *you* every time she opens her eyes and smiles?"

Don't.

"She has your hair and fingernails, Julien."

He flashed her an all-encompassing glance, reminding her too late of her mistake. The fact that she'd been looking for resemblances of him in their daughter proved that she wasn't indifferent to him no matter how much she tried to pretend otherwise.

"It's her beautiful face I'm talking about," Julien added in a quiet voice. "Clair continually scolds me because I dote on her more than the boys. Poor Clair. I don't suppose she's ever known a love like ours, so she couldn't possibly understand."

"Julien," Tracey blurted, anxious to get off such a dangerous subject, "about Clair and the other nannies—I realize you couldn't possibly have gotten along without them. But now that Dr. Simoness has given me a clean bill of health, I want to take care of the children myself."

His long, well-shaped fingers suddenly tightened on the steering wheel so the knuckles stood out white, an indication of the depth of emotion he was experiencing.

"I'd hoped you'd feel that way," he said in thick tones. "We'll ask them to join us for dinner this evening, then tell them their services are no longer required."

On that note, he double-clutched the Ferrari, causing it to fairly leap onto the main road while Tracey craned her head for some sight of the children.

Always a step ahead of her, Julien murmured, "They took the path to the lake. If it's this warm tomorrow, we'll ask Cook to prepare a picnic and we'll take our children on a boat ride."

"That would be wonderful," she burst out excitedly before realizing her mistake. To cover her tracks, she quickly added, "But we'd have to buy some little life preservers first."

"I took care of that a long time ago in anticipation of this day."

Julien sounded happy. *Too happy.* It broke Tracey's heart all over again.

"After our visit to Dr. Chappuis, we'll go to La Fermière for lunch. It's been a long time since you enjoyed raclette."

Raclette. Their favorite potato dish, covered with cheese fondue flavored with the cherry brandy called kirsch. There was nothing quite like it, but that was probably because she'd always eaten it with Julien. He made every experience magical.

The problem was, it would do no good to tell him she didn't want to have lunch or dinner or anything else with him. Along with his desire to see her gain back the weight she'd lost, his determination to be a real family—to make their marriage work within the thirty-day time period—was a fact of life she had to accept.

The only thing to do was go along with him and treat him like a good friend.

A good friend was all he could be to her now.

"That sounds nice," she said, trying to keep her voice level.

Though he said nothing, she felt his rapier glance, which penetrated the surface to the troubled woman beneath the facade.

Her body shrank from that look because it meant that Julien intended to do everything possible to break her down. He'd let nothing stop him, but he was up against something beyond his power to fix.

Within the month, he'd realize she was incapable of passion. Then, and only then, would he be forced to let her go....

"Dr. Chappuis is back from the hospital and will see you now."

With trepidation, Tracey turned to her husband, not liking what she had to do. But there was no other way.

"Julien, if you don't mind, I'd like to go in alone. Up until now, you've been doing everything for me, treating me as if I'm an invalid or something. I—I want to feel like I'm a viable person again, independent," she murmured. "You *do* understand what I'm trying to say?"

A devastating bleakness extinguished the light from his eyes.

Another wound. One of many she would be inflicting over the next twenty-eight days.

With an almost imperceptible nod of his dark head, he granted his consent, standing immobile while she followed the nurse from the reception area on legs that felt as insubstantial as water. Thankful when she could no longer feel his gaze on her retreating back, she hurried toward the pediatrician's private office.

Dr. Chappuis looked to be in his sixties, a short, smiling, gentle man who put her at ease and seemed genuinely happy to meet the recovered coma victim and lovely mother of the famous Chappelle triplets.

Before she could ask any questions, he'd shown her to a seat opposite his desk, then proceeded to assure her that her babies were in perfect health and progressing beautifully.

Since Julien had told her as much, the doctor's words came as no surprise. Still, the wonderful news was like a balm to her soul.

After he'd finished going over each of the children's charts with her, he assumed she was satisfied and rose to his feet, obviously assuming their visit was over.

That's when Tracey found the courage to look up at him and tell him the truth of the situation. After swearing him to secrecy, she explained the reason why she'd run away from Julien in the first place, the reason for her temporary amnesia, *and* the reason why she was here now—because she needed to know the triplets' prognosis and be prepared for future medical problems.

In an instant, Dr. Chappuis's beaming face was replaced by a shocked, pained expression. Slowly he sat back down, staring at her with the same kind of compassion she'd felt from Louise.

"In a case like yours," he began after clearing his throat, "there really aren't any tests to be run, not for chromosome damage. We'll simply have to wait and watch for mental retardation, which, *if* it's going to show up, probably won't be evident for several more years." After a pause, he added, "If it's any consolation, to this point in their development, your children have progressed within the normal limits."

So far they were all right. That was something to be thankful for!

Tracey's eyes closed tightly. From here on out, she'd live one day at a time caring for her dear babies and be grateful. The future she would leave to God.

Another fierce rush of longing to hold them in her arms had her practically leaping from the chair. Proffering her thanks for everything he'd done for the children, she left Dr. Chappuis's office.

As she rounded the corner to the reception area, she almost ran into Julien. It took every ounce of willpower not to fling herself in his arms.

He caught her hands, rubbing her wrists with his thumbs. "What's wrong, *mignonne*?" His dark eyes made a clinical appraisal of her features. "Your pulse is racing too fast to be healthy."

Because of you, Julien. All because of you.

"After talking to the doctor, I'm so anxious to get back to the children I don't want to waste another second," she assured him not untruthfully and eased her hands away. "Can we go to La Fermière another day?"

His eyes narrowed as if he was still looking for that elusive something. Tracey's limbs trembled because Julien possessed uncanny powers of perception and she didn't know how long she could keep up this facade.

"I only suggested it in case you weren't quite ready to undertake the strenuous task of mothering three children at once," he murmured.

"I'm more than ready."

For the moment, her unequivocal statement seemed to satisfy him. "Then we'll go straight home."

Armed with a lot of new information provided by the doctor, she found it easy enough to keep the conversation focused on the children as Julien drove them back to the château. Anyone listening would have thought they were the typical married couple, discussing the ups and downs of raising their offspring.

But every once in a while she would cast a furtive glance at Julien because she couldn't help herself. Then she would remember how *untypical* they were, and she'd feel crucified all over again because *she still wanted him with every breath in her body*.

Terrified of her feelings for Julien that, to her chagrin, seemed to be growing stronger instead of the other way around, she jumped from the car the second he pulled up in front of the château. He hadn't even shut off the engine before she let herself in the front doors.

One of the maids greeted her as she bounded up the curving staircase. Tracey called back to her but didn't pause in stride as she raced toward the children's bedrooms on the second floor.

Not used to the exertion, she entered the first door on her right out of breath, surprising one of the nannies who was in the process of changing a diaper. "Madame Chappelle!" the older woman muttered in surprise.

Tracey barely registered the astonishment on the woman's face because her attention was focused on the baby lying in the crib. He had light blond hair, his inheritance from Henri Chappelle. *But she wouldn't think about that now*.

"Which one is he?" she asked in an awestruck whisper.

"It's Raoul." Her husband's deep voice spoke from behind, startling her. "*Bon après-midi*, Jeanette."

The kind-faced woman flashed Julien a welcoming smile as she lifted the baby off the mattress so Tracey could have a better look. "He's the quieter of your two sons, *madame*, except when he's hungry. I believe he's a great thinker, and reminds me the most of your husband."

Her words caught Tracey off guard. For five out of the six months, this woman had been Raoul's mother. Naturally she would notice everything. The knowledge filled Tracey with a terrible envy.

"*Raoul!*"

CHAPTER SIX

THE name of her baby had barely passed her lips before she reached for him, hardly able to believe that this robust, chunky, pink-cheeked son had been the one at risk, the one she'd almost lost.

Raoul's struggle for breath during the first few weeks of his life had bonded her to him in a very special way. Tracey remembered the hours she'd spent in the preemie unit hovering over him, willing him to start breathing on his own.

"My little sweetheart," she crooned, her voice catching as she drew him into her arms.

Tracey lost count of the next few minutes as she alternately kissed and squeezed him, then examined every inch of his roly-poly body.

Miraculously the baby let her pour out her affection without trying to wriggle away. But his black eyes, which mirrored Julien's and now were studying her face with that keen attentiveness so characteristic of her husband's, made Tracey gasp.

As the inevitable sobs welled up, she tried to stifle them against Raoul's shirt-clad tummy. That's when he started to cry, no doubt because she'd frightened him.

In an effort to repair the damage, she propped him against her shoulder and rocked him back and forth, shaping her hand against his head to memorize the sweet feel of him. "Forgive me, Raoul. Mommy's sorry. It's just that I love you so much," she whispered over and over again, but he wouldn't be comforted.

"Before you picked him up, he was hungry for his lunch," Jeanette interjected. "I think he's like a lot of men who get a little grumpy before they're fed."

Her comment plus the twinkle in her eye made Tracey feel better. Still, it was hard to relinquish Raoul to the older woman's care.

Julien kissed the top of his blond head before he said, "While you attempt to satisfy that insatiable appetite, *mon fils*, your mother and I are going to see what our firstborn has to say for himself."

Though Julien hadn't been there in the beginning, he seemed to know everything about their children, about the precarious circumstances of her delivery, even the order in which the children had been born, with Valentine in the middle.

After the complicated procedure, Dr. Learned had explained to Tracey that because Raoul had come out last, he may have been the one with the least amount of room in her womb, which could have accounted for his underdeveloped lungs.

But he was certainly making up for them now. Tracey could hear his wails the second she followed Julien from the nursery. After all that attention focused on him, he must have felt abandoned.

Tracey didn't envy Jeanette, who had to try to calm him down before she could feed him. Naturally Tracey wanted to be the one to do everything for her precious baby, but until she held her other son in her arms, she wouldn't know any peace.

Avoiding Julien's eyes because all her emotions were spilling over right now, she ran ahead of him and opened the next door along the corridor.

When she entered the nursery, the nanny, whom Julien addressed as Lise, looked up in surprise and greeted them. But all Tracey's attention centered on her other son, who was being fed in his swing.

Though he, too, had inherited blond hair that was somewhat darker than Raoul's, his olive complexion and physical likeness to Julien shouted at her. Here was the son who with his leaner body and long limbs would look the most like his father when he grew to maturity.

Without stopping to consider the consequences, Tracey raced over to him and got down on her knees, anxious to see the color of his eyes, which were a definite hazel and heavily lashed, much like her own. Apparently he'd been eating squash and plums because traces of both remained on his upper lip.

"Oh, Jules!" Tears pooled in Tracey's eyes. "How adorable you are." Unable to resist, she cupped his handsome face in her hands and began kissing him, food and all.

But Jules wasn't having any of it and burst into tears, reaching for Julien, who quickly extricated him from the swing and quieted him down.

The baby kept hiding his face in Julien's neck, obviously a familiar position, holding on to his father for dear life. Tracey circled them and tried to get her son's attention, but he jerked his head the other way as if he were terrified she'd try to hold him.

On an intellectual level, Tracey understood his reaction. The problem was, she was too full of feelings—too eager to make up for the past half year—to view his behavior as anything but rejection.

Julien knew exactly what she was experiencing because he murmured, "While I calm him down, why not go see if Valentine has finished her lunch?"

Tracey didn't want to leave, but what choice did she have? If she stayed in the room, Jules would refuse to look at her or finish his food. This was hardly the way she expected their first reunion to go.

After nodding to Julien, she left in search of their daughter, thankful that Raoul hadn't turned away from her at first sight, or she probably wouldn't have been able to handle it.

When she entered Valentine's room, she discovered Clair fitting her dark-haired baby girl into a pink velour sleeper outfit with feet.

After the experience with Jules, Tracey approached her daughter cautiously. "Has she had her lunch?'' she whispered to Clair. Like radar, Valentine's tiny shell ears picked up on it and she turned her head in Tracey's direction.

Clair nodded. ''She ate half her lamb and all her apricots. Now she's ready for bed and a bottle. Would you like to give it to her?''

''If she'll let me,'' Tracey murmured in a shaky voice.

''Let's find out. Sit down.''

After Tracey did her bidding, the nanny handed her the baby. At first, Valentine squirmed a little and made a few sounds of protest. But the second Tracey took the bottle from Clair and put the nipple in the baby's mouth, she settled down and started drinking.

''Valentine, darling,'' she crooned to her daughter.

All the while the baby sucked and made loud breathing noises, her green eyes stared into Tracey's as if she recognized their color and could see beneath the surface.

Was it possible Valentine remembered the sound of her mother's voice, her fragrance?

For the whole month of her hospital stay, Tracey had held all three babies exactly like this. Could *that* be the reason why Valentine unexpectedly relaxed against her?

The beautiful oval face looking up at her so trustingly would have thrilled any mother, but no one more than Tracey, who hugged this child to her heart.

Suddenly Valentine wasn't enough. Tracey needed to be with all her children.

Responding to a mother's instinct, she got up from the chair and left the room with Valentine still cuddled in her arms. She headed directly for Raoul's room and upon entering was glad to see he hadn't finished his bottle or fallen asleep.

"Jeanette?" she called to the nanny who was cleaning up the lunch mess. "Would you please ask one of the maids to get a big comforter from off one of the beds and bring it in here?"

Though the older woman looked puzzled by the request she said, "Of course," and immediately left the room. While Tracey waited, she went over to Raoul's crib and cupped his rounded cheek with her free hand.

In response, his mouth let go of the nipple and his left hand reached up to touch her fingers. She put out her pinky and he clung to it, trying to put it in his mouth.

"*Voilà, madame.*"

"Would you mind putting it on the chair, Jeanette? Then you and Clair are free to do whatever you'd like for the rest of the day." Tracey sensed the nanny's surprise and felt forced to explain, "I need time with my children."

"Very well, *madame*. But we won't be far in case you get too tired."

It was difficult for Tracey to tell if Jeanette's reluctance to leave her post stemmed from her attachment to the baby, or her concern for Tracey's health. Perhaps it was a little of both.

Certainly if Tracey had been the one caring for Raoul all this time, she would have loved him so much that when the moment came, she wouldn't have been able to give him up.

More than ever, Tracey was determined that the nannies be relieved of their jobs and allowed to find work elsewhere. She had the grace to feel sorry for them because she knew they'd never be employed by anyone as kind and as fair as Julien.

Relieved when the door closed, Tracey went over to the crib and placed Valentine inside next to Raoul. For a few minutes, she smiled down at her two children, whose eyes never left her face while they held their own bottles and finished drinking.

Taking advantage of the quiet, she reached for the comforter and spread it near the crib on top of the wall-to-wall carpeting Julien had had installed, probably to make the upstairs rooms warmer.

When that was accomplished, she took off her shoes and jacket, left them on the chair, then lifted Raoul from the crib and laid him on the quilt, tummy-side down. She did the same with Valentine, then assumed the identical position on the quilt so she could watch and touch them both without having to move.

The next few minutes felt like pure bliss to Tracey, who continually kissed them, rubbed their backs and talked to them about her plans for their future.

"Well, well, Jules," came a low, familiar voice from the doorway, quickening Tracey's senses so her heart began its painful hammering. "It looks like my family is having a caucus. Shall we join them and find out what's going on?"

Before she could countenance it, Julien had plopped Jules on his stomach between Valentine and Raoul, then extended his own masculine length next to Tracey so the five of them were in touching distance of each other.

Julien could have no idea how his nearness affected her. As for Jules, he wasn't happy about the situation, either, but his misery stemmed from being separated from his father.

Out of a sense of preservation and the desire to comfort her son, Tracey inched her way forward and started playing with Jules's long fingers whose square-shaped ends were exactly like his father's. He didn't want to accept her ministrations, but Tracey kept speaking in soothing tones to him and he finally stopped his fussing.

Her head was close enough for her other babies to pull the ash blond strands of her hair and try to put them in their mouths. Yet while that part felt so right, her body could sense the warmth radiating from Julien, who lay far too close to her. The male tang from his body combined with the scent of the soap he used in the shower teased her nostrils and nearly drove her mad.

To cover her emotions, she reached for Jules, then turned on her back so she could play with him by lifting him in the air and kissing his tummy. The other two children still held on to her hair, not seeming in the least upset she was paying attention to their brother.

But as soon as she made Jules laugh out loud, she realized her mistake because by now Julien had turned on his side to watch her.

Tracey recognized the stillness that had come over him. She didn't have to see into his eyes to know the fires that blazed beneath those shuttered lids.

Though he did nothing overt—nothing she could accuse him of—his desire reached out for her like a living thing, intensifying the danger of being this close to him.

His mere presence triggered such an over-whelming response in Tracey, she was forced to turn on her side, away from temptation.

Using Jules as a human shield, she cuddled her baby against her trembling body and began singing a lullaby. Perhaps it was the music that calmed him because he let her kiss and love him, just like her other babies.

The bittersweet moment caused hot tears of joy and pain to trickle from the corners of her eyes. Joy because her fulfillment as a mother was so great. But it came at a price that brought nothing but soul-destroying pain. Lying next to her was the man she loved more than her own life. The one man denied to her from birth, *if* she had but known it.

She knew it now.

Still, a part of her rebelled against this ghastly new knowledge that had literally torn her world to pieces. Part of her wanted to ignore everything and go on loving Julien as if Henri Chappelle had never spoken.

But God knew her terrible secret, and He knew that *she* knew it. There was no hiding place, no limbo where she and Julien could go to live out the rest of their days.

Indescribable sadness pierced her breast as she pressed her wet face against Jules's sweet-smelling nape. From here on out, her children would have to be her only comfort, her *raison d'être*.

"Mignonne?"

No. Please. No. Don't talk. Don't say anything.

But it was too late. He *had* spoken. Tracey groaned because there was no mistaking the urgency or the huskiness in her husband's voice as he called softly to her.

"Months ago, when things looked their darkest, I used to dream about moments like this...ensconced in my own home, surrounded by my children, my wife....

"How is it possible you can lie here next to me and our babies and not feel what I'm feeling? Not want this to go on forever?

"Tell me, *mon amour—if* you can. Convince me that you don't belong in my arms, that you don't hunger for the kind of rapture we shared up until the very second you disappeared from my life," he entreated, his voice throbbing. "*Tracey...*"

Everything he was feeling, everything she couldn't—wouldn't—allow him to say, was alive in that one pleading word of endearment.

Her soul felt murdered all over again. Out of self-preservation, the only thing to do was lie there and feign sleep.

Oh, to be one of her babies, all of whom had drifted into slumber and had no worries.

Each moment that passed now was pure agony because Tracey knew that Julien was waiting for the slightest sign that she'd heard him, that she wanted and needed him as much as he wanted and needed her.

She couldn't possibly respond and found herself praying harder than she'd ever prayed in her life. To her immense relief, her body finally started to relax until she knew no more.

When next she became cognizant of her surroundings, she felt a weight across her hips. In her somnolent state, she assumed Jules had somehow climbed over her. Without conscious thought, she felt for him, wanting to touch his silky hair with her palm and assure herself that he was really there.

But she knew something was wrong the instant her hand came in contact with the head nestled against her breast. The features were too prominent, the hair too vibrant and crisp to be Jules.

Her eyes flew open and she had to bite her lip to keep from crying out.

Somehow during her nap, she'd let go of Jules, who was still sleeping as soundly as her other babies, and had turned toward Julien, who had also drifted off.

What wasn't possible when she was conscious, had happened while they'd slept. Instinctively she and Julien had reached for each other. His arm had caught her around the hip in a possessive hold, while her arms had enfolded his head and shoulders just as greedily.

While Tracey was still trying to recover, never mind figure out a way to get up without disturbing her husband, Clair chose that moment to peek inside the room. But just as quickly she went away again, obviously realizing she'd interrupted something very intimate and personal between husband and wife.

Tracey could imagine what construction the nanny would put on what she thought she saw. No doubt she'd tell the others.

When Tracey looked down, she saw that her blouse was badly wrinkled and that it had come loose from the waistband of her skirt. Not only that, Julien's arm had made the material ride up her legs, exposing more than was decent of her silk-clad thighs.

Embarrassment consumed Tracey along with a scorching sense of guilt. White-hot heat filled her cheeks.

This should never have happened, could never be allowed to happen again.

Twenty-seven more torturous days to get through and already one of her worst fears had come to fruition.

In absolute panic, she backed away from him, hoping he wouldn't wake up. But she'd forgotten Jules, who was in her path and didn't like the sudden jostling his mother's backside gave him. He let out a loud cry of distress that brought everyone awake. Almost instantly the other two joined in the ruckus.

Full of remorse, Tracey got to her feet as fast as she could, but not fast enough to escape Julien, whose eyes opened the moment he felt her slip from his embrace. The triumphant message in those dark depths told her he knew exactly what had happened while they'd been asleep.

He'd been waiting for such a sign. Now she'd given it to him and there was no denying it.

Knowing how Julien's mind worked filled her with terror. Armed with this new knowledge, he'd use it until he broke her down completely.

In a frantic move, she swept Raoul in her arms. Oddly enough *he* was crying the hardest, so she carried him over to his crib to change his diaper. She found his pacifier and inserted it in his mouth, crooning softly to him. It seemed to do the trick and his tears stopped.

By now the noise had abated because Julien had picked up the other two. As he went out the door, she heard him say, "Let's give your mother some time with your brother. Soon it will be your turn.

She's home to stay, *mes enfants*, and we'll have the rest of our lives to be together."

No, Julien. We won't. Not the way you mean.

"The children have always liked drives in the car, but I believe they're enjoying the boat more. What do you think?"

Clever Julien, sticking to the children as the topic of conversation, never once touching on anything personal, never referring to that scene in Raoul's bedroom yesterday when she'd been caught holding her husband in her arms.

"Since this is all so new to me, I have no way of knowing such a thing, but they do seem content."

All three infants lay propped in their carryalls on the floor behind Julien, who handled the controls of the sleek twenty-one-foot ski boat. Avoiding even a glance in his direction, Tracey watched her babies play with their hands and bite on a few rattles Julien had brought along from their toy bin.

Besides their life preservers and stretchy suits with feet, they wore sky blue cotton sweaters. Tracey pulled up the hoods to cover their ears and head. Only their precious faces were exposed to the warm afternoon sun that took the fall nip out of the air.

When she wasn't feeding them or changing their diapers, she'd reach for them one at a time and cuddle them. As they cruised around the placid lake, she'd point out a famous landmark like the medieval Château de Chillon or the water jet in Geneva's harbor.

At one place near the shoreline at the Château de Clarens, an old fossil of a fortress, Julien cut the engine to get himself something to eat from the cooler. The cook had prepared mouth-watering quiches, *tartes aux framboises*, and she'd supplied them with Grapillon, a grape drink Tracey adored.

While her eyes scanned the hillsides teeming with vineyards full of ripe grapes ready to be harvested, he fixed a plate for Tracey, then himself, and they ate in what must have looked like companionable silence. But inside, she was a seething mass of nerves.

In an effort to break the tension, she said, "You were very generous to the nannies last night when you told them that we were letting them go. I'm sure they're grateful, Julien."

He swallowed another tart before replying, "There's not enough money in this world to recompense them for mothering the children until you could take over. But I have to admit that for their sakes, I'm glad they've been forced to move on. Jeanette, particularly, was too attached to Raoul."

Tracey nodded. "I sensed as much yesterday. He's so sweet." Her voice choked up and her eyes filled as she looked at her children. "They're all so sweet."

"They're perfect, and today I feel as if I'm the luckiest man alive," he murmured with gut-wrenching emotion.

"Julien," she blurted, anxious to cut him off before he led them into deeper waters, "I—I hope you won't mind that I called Isabelle early this morning and—''

"Why in heaven's name would I mind?" he bit out unexpectedly, revealing that he wasn't as in control as she had imagined. "This is your home now, and she's your sister after all."

Clutching her hands together, she said, "You didn't let me finish. I haven't seen her or Alex in half a year and I'm afraid he'll forget me, s-so I've invited them to come and stay at the château with us for a while."

Not by the twitch of a facial muscle did Julien reveal his true feelings on the matter. Instead, he bit into his quiche, then asked in a bland voice, "Do you think that's wise after what Rose told us at dinner last night?"

Tracey sucked in her breath. "You're talking about Bruce."

"Tracey—" Julien frowned "—he doesn't know the meaning of work. Being a guest at the château will only set him back further."

"I know," she whispered. "That's why my invitation didn't include him. Rose and I talked after we put the babies to bed. She agrees with me that maybe it's depression over Bruce, rather than morning sickness, that is getting her down. Maybe a few weeks here, playing with the babies and getting out of herself by spending time with Angelique, will be good therapy. Isabelle needs to be with family right now," she added not untruthfully.

But her real reason for inviting her sister to Lausanne was to widen the gulf between herself and Julien, and he knew it.

"How soon would you like her to come?"

"As soon as arrangements can be made."

"Then I'll see to her airline tickets when we get back from boating."

"No, Julien." At her rejection of his offer, his head reared back and she knew she'd angered him. "I—I mean, she'll take care of that herself."

"How?" he demanded a trifle aggressively.

"She still has some savings."

"Then she needs to hold on to them."

"Daddy left that money for her. I told her to use it. Bruce needs a rude awakening, or he'll end up destroying their marriage."

The minute the words left her mouth, she knew she'd said the wrong thing and wanted to die. In the damning silence that followed, the color drained out of Julien's face, leaving it an expressionless mask.

"Would it be all right if I took the boat back to Lausanne?" she asked, trying to change the subject to cover her pain. "I know it's been a long time, but since there's no wind, I think I can handle it."

"There was never any doubt of that, *mignonne*," he replied in a deceptively mild voice. "But since the children and I aren't ready to go home yet, why don't you head for Évian?" Inherent in his seemingly innocent question was a command, one she had to obey without remonstration or she'd give herself away.

Tracey's heart sank to her feet. Évian was on the French side of the lake. It suited Julien to be gone several more hours, hours in which she would have to think up new ways to keep her emotional distance from him.

After yesterday, she didn't dare show him how vulnerable she was and had to comply with his wishes. But her hands were unsteady on the gears as she raised the anchor and started up the motor.

"Better switch to the other tank," he reminded her because she'd forgotten. "We'll fill up again when we reach the opposite shore."

Except for the humming sound of the engine, nothing else broke the silence as they skimmed across the pale blue water. It appeared they had the lake to themselves. Not even the occasional wake from another boat made so much as a ripple on top of the glasslike surface.

Looking back over the years, she recalled there'd been other days much like today—before Henri Chappelle's confession—when Tracey had come out in the boat with Julien and found inestimable joy just by being in his company, by getting close to him.

She fought tears because she had an idea that Julien was remembering those heavenly times, too. But such moments of innocence were gone forever, could never be repeated. She felt crucified all over again at the cruel reality of their situation.

Julien had insisted she stay with him for a month in order to prove that she wanted out of her marriage. But she was fast coming to the conclusion that she'd break before the thirty days were up. If Isabelle's visit didn't produce the desired results, Tracey didn't know what she was going to do.

Telling Julien the bald truth might change him beyond recognition. Tracey realized the disillusionment and pain wouldn't kill him—he was too strong a character for that—but something inside him would shrivel up and die. He'd no longer be the same Julien everyone admired and loved.

No, no matter how many times she went over it in her mind, she always came back to her original conclusion—that he should not be told the truth. Much better that he suffer from a broken heart rather than try to function with a murdered soul.

So deep were her black thoughts, it wasn't until Julien moved her aside with firm hands and physically took over the handling of the boat that she realized he'd been trying to get her attention.

Shivering from his touch, which she felt through her windbreaker, she hurried back to the children.

"If we pull in over there," he called over his broad shoulder, pointing to a dock in the distance, "they'll gas up the boat while we go inside the restaurant. It has a new owner and they prepare the best white fish along the lake."

"But the babies—" Tracey gasped quietly, attempting to drum up any excuse that would prevent her from being alone with him much longer.

"They'll have infant chairs."

"Julien—"

"Humor me, *mignonne*. I've waited long enough for the day when I could take my family out to dinner," he murmured in a faraway voice. "That day is here, and I intend to celebrate it."

CHAPTER SEVEN

IN THIS kind of mood, Julien was invincible. She had no choice but to go along with his wishes.

Once they'd tied up to the dock, he gave instructions to the man running the gas concession, then turned to Tracey. "If you'll carry Valentine, I'll bring the boys." Assisting her out of the boat, he handed her the baby, sans carryall or life preserver.

Within seconds, he'd joined her, his strong arms around Raoul and Jules. Together, they walked the length of the dock to the shoreside restaurant.

Evening was fast approaching. The outdoor section of the sloping terrace looked particularly inviting with tables set beneath its lighted torches.

As far as Tracey could tell, most of the diners were dressed in stylish evening clothes. She felt totally out of place wearing Levi's and tennis shoes. As for Julien, he looked magnificent in anything he wore, particularly the white turtleneck layered with a navy pullover over khakis.

Wherever they went, her husband always drew attention, especially from women. But now that they were carrying three babies who were obviously triplets, every head in the place turned and people started clapping.

Out of deference to the children, the headwaiter showed them to a table inside the restaurant where they'd be warm. He snapped his fingers to the other waiters, who hustled to find infant seats. Before Tracey could sit down, dozens of people had approached her to comment on their adorable babies.

If she'd known about Julien's surprise plans, she would have done something with her hair rather than leaving it tied back with a scarf at the nape.

Casting a furtive glance at Julien, she was awed by the smile of pride and satisfaction on his handsome face, the light radiating from his eyes. He was happy, eager to show off his family to people who recognized him and couldn't seem to keep from touching the children and asking questions.

The Chappelle name was an institution in Europe and Julien was its dynamic head, but few people knew him the way Tracey did. Being with his family on an outing meant more to him than all the accolades heaped upon him by the corporate world.

That's why she couldn't tell him the truth about his father! *Their* father. Joy would go out of him. The light in his eyes would dim and his smile would fade forever. She couldn't do that to him!

Suddenly Julien's gaze locked with Tracey's, a dark, brooding look she couldn't escape. Helping her to be seated, he rasped, "I know your feelings about being married to me, but for the children's sake, pretend to enjoy this evening, *petite*."

She heard so many things in his voice—pain, rage, abject frustration. *It was killing her as surely as it was him*.

The rest of the evening passed by in a kind of blur. Tracey put up the best front she could and ate her food though her appetite had deserted her. But by the time their dessert had been brought to the table, the babies had started to fuss. After receiving a surfeit of attention, it was apparent they needed their beds. As far as Tracey was concerned, it was a miracle they'd been good this long.

Julien must have come to the same conclusion. In a quiet aside, he murmured, "I think we'll have to enjoy our *galette au chocolat* another time. Shall we go?"

Relief filled her system and she nodded. For the past hour, she'd felt like she'd been caught in a trap with all eyes upon her, upon them. At least in the boat it would be dark and Julien would have to drive, leaving her free to deal with the children and her fears.

The night air was decidedly cold now that the sun was gone. Clouds she hadn't noticed before obscured the stars. No conversation passed their lips as she followed a remote Julien from the restaurant to the dock. Once they'd settled the children in the boat, he reached for the top. By tacit agreement, she helped him snap everything in place to make the interior warm and snug for the cruise home.

Some workers on the dock who'd been discussing an approaching storm helped them cast off. Julien drove out of the harbor at an almost wakeless speed.

"Ready?"

Tracey shivered at his clipped tone. "One second." She'd decided to hold Jules because he cried every time she started to put him in his carryall. The minute she settled him on her lap he quieted down. "All right. You can go now."

With a change of gears, the boat leaped forward and flew across the water. A wind had sprung up out of nowhere, causing the waves to buffet them somewhat. But with Julien at the helm, Tracey didn't give it a thought. In fact, the steady slam of the hull breaking each wave seemed to put the children to sleep.

They might have traveled another five minutes before she felt the boat lose speed and start to turn around.

"What's happening?" she called out, forgetting her vow to leave him alone.

"The storm is building in intensity. By the time we reach the middle of the lake, it will feel like a hurricane. If we didn't have the children, I'd keep going. But I refuse to put my family at risk so we're going to head back to shore and wait it out."

No! Tracey's heart cried. But she'd known Julien for too many years. Once he'd made up his mind about something, that was it. Besides, he'd lived by the lake all his life and she trusted his judgment completely. If he thought their predicament could be in the least life threatening, then she didn't dare argue with him. The babies were his first priority.

How she loved him for the kind of man he was. No other man of her acquaintance could touch him. No man ever would. . . .

Pressing her lips to Jules's blond head, she listened to the rain hitting the windshield like spatter paint. Soon it was coming down in sheets and Julien had to use every bit of his considerable strength to keep the boat under control.

But since he thrived on challenge, no one kept a cooler head or a steadier hand. She would always be able to count on him, especially in a crisis. Anyone else would be panicked by now, but not her darling Julien.

"He'll find us a safe place," she whispered to Jules, who was still awake but had stopped crying. No doubt the noise of the storm had become more interesting to him than the sound of his own voice.

While she rocked him back and forth, her eyes sought Valentine's and Raoul's sleeping forms in the darkness. Tracey envied them because they were as blissfully unaware of the elements as they were of the tragedy created by their grandparents' lies of omission.

Like a never-ending stream, tears coursed down Tracey's cheeks. For the thousandth time, she asked herself why Henri hadn't died before she and Julien returned from their honeymoon. A few days would have made all the difference to their lives. She and

Julien could have enjoyed their marriage without ever knowing the circumstances that now forced them apart.

How could Henri have done this to them? Why hadn't her mother ever said one word? Why had she never raised a cry of warning to her daughter when she could see that Tracey had fallen under Julien's spell?

What possessed their parents to continue forcing the two families together for all those years when they were party to a secret that if revealed, threatened the very fabric of both families' existence?

"It doesn't make sense," she found herself moaning aloud.

"Tracey?"

She heard real anxiety in Julien's voice and her head flew back. "Yes?" she said, frantically dashing at the tears with her arm.

"Are you all right?"

No. I'm not. I'll never be again.

"I—I'm fine," came her tremulous response. "H-how are you?"

He didn't say anything right away, making her uneasy. The tension between them was much worse than the elements playing havoc with the boat. When he finally spoke, it was in a grating voice and her heart started to thud.

"Do you realize that's the first personal question you've asked me since you awakened from your coma?"

Tracey could feel his pain, but was incapable of responding for fear she'd give in to the impulse to tell him everything. Then it would all be over and Julien's life would change forever.

He started to say something else, then bit out an unintelligible epithet because the hull suddenly grated against a sandbar, bringing the boat to a lurching stop.

Tracey practically slid off the seat, but caught herself in time. Unfortunately, Jules started to cry at being jostled so rudely. As for Raoul, his carryall tipped on its side.

Though he landed on a padded quilt Julien had placed there in the event of such an occurrence—so they couldn't get hurt—the baby cried out in fright. This immediately awakened Valentine and within seconds all three children were crying.

While Julien climbed out the side of the boat to pull it higher up on the beach, Tracey got down on the floor to right Raoul's carryall and put Jules in his. After kissing each little flushed face, she rummaged in the cooler for their bottles.

Thank heavens for baby bottles that could go anywhere and live through anything, she mused. By the time Julien had secured the boat with ropes and had returned, the children were noisily drinking. Tracey sat in the midst of them and let them hold on to her hands with their tiny fingers, thereby reassuring them that she hadn't left them alone in the darkness.

"Do you think the hull was damaged?" she asked Julien while he made up beds for them from the padded seats running down both sides of the boat.

"Possibly to the paint, but nothing structural."

"Where are we?"

"A half mile south of the restaurant on someone's private stretch of beach. We'll be safe here until the storm passes."

If only their lives could be as simple.

"*Mon Dieu.* This is hardly the way I planned this evening to end."

"You can't order the elements around as easily as your employees," she teased so he wouldn't be so hard on himself.

"Obviously not," came the dry retort, reminiscent of other conversations in the past when there had been no threat to their happiness. "Tracey—" the longing she heard when he said her name always made her pulse race "—I'll take over with the children now. After this ordeal, you should lie down and get some rest."

"No, Julien," she stated in a firm voice. "You're the one who needs the respite. For months you've had the responsibility for the whole family on your shoulders. You deserve a night off. Let me watch over them while *you* sleep. I need to bond with them so they won't miss their nannies too much. I want them to love me," she said, her voice catching.

Although he was lying down with his head near the steering wheel, she heard his quick intake of breath. "You bonded with them during their first month, the most crucial time of all. They got the start they needed. As for loving you, could you be in any doubt after the way they clung to you tonight at the restaurant?''

They *had* clung to her. But because her thoughts were so tied up with Julien, she hadn't stopped to analyze the children's behavior at dinner. They'd reached for her as much as for Julien when strangers put their faces too close or wanted to hold them.

''Thank you for those words.'' Her voice choked up. ''You've been so wonderful,'' she admitted, hiding her burning cheeks against Raoul's tummy.

''You can still say that when I'm holding you hostage until your thirty days are up?''

In an instant, the bitterness was back. What frightened Tracey was to hear his pain, except that it was more than pain now. Rage was growing alongside it, the one destructive emotion she hadn't thought him capable of. She couldn't bear to see what was happening to him.

''Julien—''

''I thought you were giving me the night off,'' he interrupted brutally. ''I've decided to hold you to your word.''

On that acid note he turned away, bringing an abrupt end to their conversation. She should have been relieved. She *was* relieved that he would let her take care of the children while he caught up on some much needed sleep. But she knew her continued silence over the reason for wanting a divorce was tearing him apart.

Which hell was preferable? The one he was living in now, or the new one her confession would create? Was Louise right? Would not knowing the truth drive Julien over the edge?

Throughout the rest of the night, long after the storm had passed over leaving everything as peaceful as before, Tracey sat with her arms around her babies, debating what to do. When morning came, she was still in agony and no closer to reaching a decision.

Upon awakening, Julien took one look at the dark shadows beneath her eyes and assumed she'd had a hard night of it with the babies. In a gravelly tone, he announced they were returning to the château with all possible haste. Once there, she was going straight to bed.

Tracey decided not to argue with him. There'd be time enough for that after she'd showered and changed into clean clothes.

What Julien didn't know was that she planned to do a little remodeling of his house. She wanted her children closer together. Remembering how much fun it had been to share a room with Isabelle while growing up, she felt her babies should enjoy the same experience.

If she put all three beds in one nursery, that would leave the middle room free for their toys and swings and the like. The third nursery could be used for Alex during her sister's stay. One of the play-pens with padding would make an acceptable bed for him.

As for the empty guest room across the hall from the nurseries, Tracey planned to move into it so she could listen for the children. Only a mother should have to sleep next to so many little bodies and voices.

Isabelle needed rest and quiet and could be ensured of a good sleep in the room next to Aunt Rose on the third floor. Julien had put her at the opposite end of the hall from their suite for the very reason that he didn't want the children disturbing her.

Tracey hoped Julien wouldn't mind the changes. Surely he realized that she'd never run away again, not now that she had her memory back and intended to devote her life to the children.

Full of plans and ideas that helped keep her mind from dwelling on the pain, she returned to the château with Julien and went straight to her room. She didn't fight him when he said that he'd bathe the babies and see to their breakfast.

If she gave in to him now, he'd eventually go to his study to do some work while the children were napping. Then would be the time she could start carrying out her schemes.

Once Solange knew the plan, she'd heartily approve and direct the maids to help with the moving. Everything could be taken care of before Julien looked in on the babies again and discovered her fait accompli.

Julien had told her this was her home. He'd given her permission to treat it as such and probably wouldn't mind the changes where the babies were concerned, particularly since the rooms were so large.

Of course, he might remain adamant that she stay in the bedroom adjoining his and offer to sleep across the hall from the babies *himself*. That would be something he'd do. But she'd just have to chance it. Hopefully when the time came, she could reason with him by virtue of the fact that she'd lost five months with the children. What better way to make up for the loss than by sleeping close to them?

The rearrangement of the rooms would bring her a measure of peace where her babies were concerned.

A voice deep inside reminded her that sleeping away from *him* would make life a little more bearable while she waited for her divorce.

Two hours later, after an invigorating shower and a fattening breakfast in the kitchen, Tracey went in search of Solange, who was busy dusting.

The second she told the housekeeper her plans, Solange clapped her hands and agreed that it was time to turn the house into a home. Always the talker, she confided to Tracey that she was glad the nannies had gone.

She threw up her hands by way of demonstration that she hadn't exactly approved of them, though she had to admit that they did take "adequate" care of *les petits enfants*.

But no one could ever take the place of their *chère maman*, and now that Tracey was back where she belonged, the house could return to normal and everyone could be happy again.

Tracey could see where this conversation was leading. Solange's loyalty to Henri and Celeste Chappelle had never been in question, but Julien was her favorite person in the world. No way did she approve of Tracey sleeping apart from him.

Which was why Tracey decided to say nothing about the change in her own sleeping arrangements. Solange would find out soon enough, and though she wouldn't like it, there wouldn't be anything she could do about it.

One of the maids enlisted to check on Julien's whereabouts returned to the kitchen to tell Solange that after putting the babies to sleep, he had gone down to the private dock with the estate manager to check out the damage to the boat.

Armed with that information, Tracey and Solange set about their tasks with a camaraderie built over many years' association because of their mutual love of one man.

As they worked side by side, Tracey tried to imagine the impact on Solange if she ever learned the truth about Julien and Tracey. Somehow she suspected it would be devastating to the family retainer.

Solange was a good Catholic. To discover that her esteemed employer had had an affair with Tracey's mother would constitute the ultimate betrayal.

The truth would bring about too much sadness for everyone involved. Tracey couldn't bear to be the one to impart it.

"Good night, my little darlings," she whispered to her children a few hours later. "Sleep well. Mommy loves you."

Tracey had held each of them to give them their bottles. Now they were snug in their sleepers and ready for bed.

She breathed a sigh of satisfaction at seeing all of them together in the same bedroom. Even with three cribs and dressers, there was still plenty of room to spare.

Their bright eyes followed her movements as she covered them with a light blanket. Every smile, every baby sound tugged at her heartstrings. She still had a hard time believing she'd given birth to all three at the same time.

They were so perfect! Of course, she had her husband to thank for their beautiful bodies and features.

"We do excellent work, don't we?"

Julien had come into the nursery without her noticing. She had no idea how long he'd been watching, but judging by his remark, his thoughts were on the same wavelength as hers.

That's the way it had always been with them. They could read each other's mind without a word passing between them. This was one of those magical times.

Holding her breath, she asked, "Do you mind my putting them together? I thought I'd try an experiment, but I can always ask the maids to help me change everything back tomorrow. It's just tha—"

"Perhaps if my parents had put Jacques and Angelique in the same room with me when we were babies," Julien broke in quietly, "the three of us would have been much closer. The château is large, and the rooms are too isolated from each other."

"That's what I was thinking." Encouraged by his acceptance of her logic, she explained what she'd planned to do with the other two nurseries.

He watched her through narrowed eyes, seeming to concentrate on her mouth as she spoke. She had the impression that he was no longer listening and her heart started to pound out of rhythm.

"The thing is," she said in a breathless voice, avoiding his unnerving gaze, "n-now that the nannies are gone, I need to be closer to the children, so—"

"We'll *both* move down to this floor," he inserted smoothly. "You choose which room across the hall you want, I'll take the other."

"But, Julien—" She panicked. This wasn't going the way it was supposed to. She'd hoped to put distance between them. Instead, they would be having more interaction than ever.

"Our children are a joint responsibility, *mignonne*. I intend to help you in every way that I can, which means we'll take turns getting up in the night when necessary." He wandered over to the doorway and flipped off the light switch. "Now that the children are in bed," he said in a low, silken tone, "why don't we start to move into our new rooms? We can help each other."

Heat crept up her face and neck. "A-actually, I've already put my things in the room across from this one."

Something flickered in the black recesses of his eyes. Once again, she'd plunged a dagger deep into his heart. Another wound that would never heal.

"Then I'll gather a few things and move into the one next to yours. Come with me and we can plan another outing for tomorrow. I thought a drive to the narcissus fields might appeal."

Stop it, Julien.

"Isabelle will be here day after tomorrow," he continued. "Since she's not a nature lover like you, we should take advantage of this time. A picnic among the flowers will be the perfect place for the children."

Don't say any more. Don't be so loving, so considerate. I know what you're trying to do, but you'll only end up with a greater heartache.

To hide their trembling, Tracey slid her hands into the pockets of her jeans. She moved farther into the hall, tortured by his nearness. "Why don't we wait until tomorrow before we make any definitive plans? If you don't mind, I'm more tired than I realized and would like to go to bed."

"That's not surprising," he murmured. "You were up all last night with our children while I slept. Tonight it will be my turn. *Bonne nuit, mon amour.*"

He opened the door to her room. Of necessity she had to step past him.

It was a mistake.

The action of her arm brushing against his chest aroused the passion that had enflamed them both on their honeymoon. Terrified that he could sense how easily his touch had turned her into a throbbing mass of need, she walked over to the phone on the bedside table and picked up the receiver.

She pretended not to know that Julien was still standing there while she dialed her sister in San Francisco. Ten o'clock Swiss time meant it was seven in the morning over there.

The second Isabelle answered, Tracey greeted her with feigned enthusiasm and burst into an excited account about the children and the arrangements she'd made for Alex once the two of them arrived.

It seemed a long time before Tracey heard the click that sounded a death knell in her heart. Julien had gone. She'd shut him out on purpose and wondered how much more he would let pass by before retaliating. Worse, she feared the form it would take. Under the circumstances, she didn't dare accompany him on that mountain picnic tomorrow.

Children or no children, anything could happen while they basked under a warm sun among the flowers. At this point, to go anywhere alone with Julien was courting disaster. It was unthinkable.

CHAPTER EIGHT

TRACEY got ready for bed and slid under the covers, wishing her sister were here right now. Haunted by the hunger she'd glimpsed in Julien's eyes, it was impossible to fall asleep. She spent the greater part of the night figuring out how to put him off. As far as she was concerned, Isabelle couldn't come soon enough.

But as it turned out, Tracey needn't have worried. At daybreak she got dressed in a skirt and blouse and hurried into the nursery to check on the children.

To her astonishment, she found Julien in his robe, his hair attractively disheveled, walking the floor with Raoul, who was running a temperature. He'd been the fussy one on their boating trip and now she knew why.

"Let me take over," she insisted, and plucked the baby from his arms. The fact that Julien allowed her to take Raoul proved just how tired he was. Yet the fatigue lines around his eyes and mouth, the shadowy rasp along his jaw, made him more appealing than ever. Tracey quickly looked away before he could discover she'd been staring at him.

Rubbing the back of his neck, he said, "A half hour ago I gave him some liquid aspirin to bring down his fever, but I'm not sure it's working."

"If his temp stays up, I'll call Dr. Chappuis's office. Why don't you go to bed? I promise to let you know if he doesn't improve."

He shook his head. "Valentine and Jules will be awake in a minute."

"Julien, millions of women around the world take care of larger families than ours every day of their lives. I'll manage just fine."

He straightened to his full, imposing height. "You're barely out of hospital and need waiting on yourself."

Darling Julien. "I'm stronger than I look, and according to my bathroom scales, I've already gained two pounds. It's true," she avowed when she saw the skepticism in his expression. "Being at the clinic gave me claustrophobia and I had no appetite. But now that I'm out, food tastes good again."

He couldn't very well refute her, not when he'd watched her consume everything on her plate at the shoreside resort.

While she stood there patting Raoul's back to comfort him, she could sense Julien's ambivalence. He was relieved about her weight gain, but hesitant to leave her with all the work.

She was prompted to say, "If you don't take care of yourself, you'll probably come down with Raoul's cold, so—"

"If he has a cold, then I've already been infected," Julien broke in dryly, "so this won't matter." Following that comment, he kissed Raoul's head, then brushed her unsuspecting mouth with his own before leaving the nursery.

Tracey reeled in shock.

It was only the briefest of contact, but she felt it to her bones and was appalled because she should never have put herself in a position where such a thing could happen. *She could never let it happen again.*

Julien's sole purpose in keeping her at the château was to find her vulnerable spot and attack. How could she have forgotten that for one instant? But as she looked into Raoul's feverish face, she realized that her worry over him had made her careless.

Hardening her resolve, she determined to take steps to ensure that the situation wouldn't be repeated before she left Julien at the end of the month.

Much as she disliked any of the children being sick, Raoul's condition had thwarted his father's plans for a mountain picnic later in the day. If she didn't miss her guess, Valentine and Jules would probably come down with the same thing before long. There'd be no outings for a while and then Isabelle would arrive, frustrating Julien's attempt to undermine her resolve to leave him, whatever the reason.

And if he knew the real reason, what then? Would he be able to turn off his feelings and see her only as a half sister? Treat her with kindness rather than passion for the rest of their days?

But Tracey already knew the answer to that. She'd lived a year with the knowledge that he was her half brother, and *nothing* had changed for her.

If anything, her desire for him was even greater than before. *Never* would she be able to think of Julien without wanting to lie in his arms and know his possession.

It would be no different for him.

That was why there was no point in telling him about their parents' affair.

She'd come back to the château to prove to him that she was no longer capable of being his wife. That was where it had to start, *and end*—even if it meant being cruel....

Tracey took one look at Isabelle and asked, ''Are you tired, Iz? There's a bench up ahead. Want to sit down?''

''Maybe for a minute. But I don't know how long Alex will last.''

Tracey's gaze darted to the children in their double strollers. For some reason, her nephew doted on Valentine and insisted on riding with her. Being an active two-year-old, the minute they'd pause to look at the ducks or the paddleboats on the lake, he'd want to climb out and run around. He didn't seem to understand that Valentine was too little to run around with him.

"If he gets too restless, I'll walk him to the car and we'll come for you and the babies. How's that?"

"That sounds good." Isabelle sat down with a heavy sigh. She was only four months pregnant, but to Tracey, she looked six. "Who would have dreamed when our school used to take afternoon walks along this promenade, that one day you and I would be here with our own children?"

"I know," Tracey murmured with bittersweet emotion. "Remember that poor tree over there with the damaged bark? The one Indra ran into with Jacques's car?"

Isabelle started to laugh. "And we had to take up a collection from everyone to get it fixed so he never found out? Where is Jacques anyway? I've been here two weeks and he's never shown his face."

"I haven't seen him, either, but I believe he's out of the country on business for the company."

"On Julien's orders, I presume. Ever since Jacques made a play for you, there's been a rift between them. Angelique says it's worse than ever."

"That was over a long time ago, Iz," Tracey defended, but suffered another guilty pang. Was it possible that Julien was purposely keeping Jacques away, thinking that he might have something to do with Tracey's desire for a divorce?

"Hey, Trace? Now that we're on the subject of Julien, how about coming clean with me? I know you're leaving him at the end of the month, but for the life of me, I can't figure out why."

"I've told you before. I don't want to be married."

Isabelle cocked her dark head, perplexed. "Are you insane? Julien worships the ground you walk on. He never saw anyone but you. I ought to know because I tried everything in my power to make him pay attention to me. He just treated me as if I were invisible. It's embarrassing to have to admit that there was a time when I hated you for your power over him."

Tracey's head swerved around and she stared at her sister in stunned surprise. "You don't mean that."

"Yes, I'm afraid I was very jealous of you in those days. So jealous I probably married Bruce right off the bat because when he met the two of us at that party in San Francisco, it was *me* he wanted, not you."

"Iz..." Tracey whispered. "I didn't know."

"Hey, that was over a long time ago—" Isabelle flashed her a reassuring smile "—and whatever his faults, I love my husband. Being separated from him has made me realize just how much. Look, Trace, the only reason I brought any of it up is because it's obvious you're tearing your husband apart. It kills me to watch. I adore Julien. Good grief, how can you ignore him the way you do? How can you stay out of his bed? That's what I want to know."

Tracey's eyes closed tightly. "I've told you. Our marriage is over and I want my freedom."

"Why? Angelique thinks maybe you're secretly afraid of getting pregnant again. But there are ways to ensure you don't have to worry about that."

"Look, I don't mean to be cruel, but it's no one else's business. Julien and I are through."

"Say that to anyone but me. As I recall, you could never get enough of him and practically had a nervous breakdown when you found out our trips to Switzerland had been called off permanently."

"That's because I was besotted. But I grew up, Iz."

She shook her head. "I don't buy it. Not for one second. You're lying, Trace, and though Julien hasn't said as much, he knows you're lying, too."

Miraculously, Alex chose that moment to climb out of his seat, forcing Tracey to jump up and grab him before he ran into the street. After giving him a kiss and a squeeze, she said, "I think your little guy has had enough. As for my babies, they need a diaper change and some dinner. Let's get back to the car."

"I'm not finished with you yet, Trace."

"Yes, you are, Iz," she muttered angrily. "*Tu comprends*?"

"Get as mad as you want, but I can see through you and I'm not about to let this go."

Tracey wheeled around, hot-faced. "Have I ever once interfered in your marital problems?"

"No," Isabelle retorted. "And heaven knows Bruce and I've got them. I think that's why I've felt so sick. Fortunately, Julien has given me some sound advice." It didn't surprise Tracey. He had always been able to get through to Isabelle when no one else could. "I'm going to try it out on Bruce when I go home tomorrow."

"That's good, but I have to confess I'm not ready to let you go yet," Tracey cried in a plaintive voice.

"I don't want to leave you, either, but last night Bruce sounded like he really missed me."

"I'm sure he does. Forgive me for being selfish. He's crazy about you and I love him for it."

"So if I were to suddenly ask Bruce for a divorce, are you telling me that you wouldn't want to know the reason why? That you wouldn't hound me for the truth?"

Though she could feel it slipping away from her, Tracey stood her ground and said, "Yes. Your marriage is your own business. I would give you credit for knowing exactly what you were doing, and I'd never presume to tell you how to run your life."

"I'm not trying to tell you anything, Trace. All I'm asking for here is a little honesty. Mom and Dad are gone. Since you refuse to confide in Aunt Rose, then use *me*. Let me help. Please." Her voice shook with emotion.

Tracey was touched by her sister's sincerity. In ways, they were closer than ever, probably because they'd both become mothers and shared common interests now. It was going to be a real wrench when she left.

But much worse, Tracey and Julien would be alone again. The thought absolutely terrified her.

She took a shallow breath. "I've told you the truth, but like Julien, you refuse to accept it. That's why I ran away the first time, because I knew he couldn't handle it. Apparently you can't, either," she said in a dull voice. "I'm sorry."

"You couldn't be as sorry as I am. What you're doing to Julien is wrong, Trace. One day you'll find out just how wrong."

Isabelle was starting to sound like Louise. Tracey couldn't deal with it anymore and took off for the car at a brisk pace, preventing further conversation.

Jules and Raoul had been asleep in the stroller, but at their mother's speedy departure, they awoke with a start and began to whimper. It couldn't be helped. Tracey didn't want Isabelle to catch up with her.

She had no desire to continue their soul-destroying confrontation, the kind only sisters who knew each other so well—who'd shared the good and the bad over a lifetime—could get involved in.

It was draining enough trying to figure out how she was going to stay away from Julien another seven days before she walked away from him for good.

As if the fates were against her, chaos developed when they arrived back at the château and Alex threw a temper tantrum because he had to be separated from Valentine.

As Isabelle carried her kicking, screaming, out-of-control son into the château, Julien emerged to help Tracey with the children. He reached for his sons, kissing them on their blond heads while Tracey plucked her daughter from the stroller.

"What's the problem?" he murmured, locking gazes with her.

"I think Valentine has become my nephew's obsession."

The minute the words left her lips, she felt as if someone had just walked over her grave.

Dear God. Was history starting to repeat itself?

Could Alex's preoccupation with his beautiful little dark-haired cousin be the beginning of a serious attachment?

Julien's eyes glowed like banked fires. "I'm not at all surprised. She takes after her mother."

His low aside produced more panic inside Tracey. If the two cousins were allowed to grow up together, would it result in a full-fledged love affair? Another family secret? Another lie with disastrous consequences?

Horrified at the prospect, Tracey unconsciously tightened her hold on her daughter until Valentine squirmed. Immediately contrite, she kissed her baby's cheek, vowing that she'd never let that happen to Valentine or the boys.

In a few more months Isabelle would deliver another son or daughter. In time both Angelique and Jacques would probably have children. Over the years there would be family get-togethers, vacations...

Tracey would have to start right now to distance her children from their relatives. She'd heard too many true accounts about first and second cousins falling in love.

Suddenly she was glad Isabelle was leaving. Much as she adored Alex, there was no way she would let him get close to Valentine.

Her tortured thoughts shot ahead. She prayed her sister's new baby wouldn't be a girl with a fatal predilection for men named Chappelle. Somehow Tracey would have to take steps to make certain that never happened!

"*Mignonne*?" Julien's anxious voice brought her back to the present. "You've gone pale. What's wrong?"

He saw too much! "Nothing that a good dinner won't fix," she rushed to assure him and started for the door.

"Somehow I don't believe you." He followed her inside the foyer. "It's because Isabelle's leaving tomorrow. Maybe what I have planned will help cheer you up."

Tracey paused on the first step and turned her head toward him. "What do you mean?"

A faint smile broke the corner of his compelling mouth. "This evening you and I are giving a going-away party in Isabelle's honor. Solange has set up everything in the main dining room."

"W-who's coming?"

"Angelique helped me draw up a list to include mutual friends. You haven't laughed or been carefree for a long, long time. I'm hoping tonight will rectify the situation, if only for a few hours."

A huge lump lodged in her throat so she could hardly swallow. Julien was a giver. He always thought of others before himself. He certainly couldn't have planned anything calculated to please Isabelle more.

But except for the joy she found in her children, there could be no laughter in Tracey's life. One day soon, Julien would realize that his marriage was a lost cause and he'd stop wishing for the impossible.

Unfortunately, she still had tonight to get through. In a small voice, she asked, "What time will our guests be arriving?"

"You have an hour to pamper yourself. Tell Isabelle to do the same. I've already instructed the maids to deal with the children and put them to bed."

"Then I'd better hurry."

Without waiting for a response, she dashed up the stairs with Valentine.

To her chagrin, instead of being able to distance herself from her husband, he'd once again put her in a position where she'd be forced to work hand in hand with him.

He knew exactly what he was doing when he told her that her only job was to get dressed up and play hostess to Angelique and a dozen of their close school friends from the past. They'd be eating in the *grande salle à manger* generally reserved for important business associates.

Tracey knew Julien's tactics better than anyone alive. He was fighting for their marriage and had deliberately placed her in a situation from which she couldn't talk or wiggle her way out without hurting her sister irreparably.

The next few hours passed in a kind of blur for Tracey, who had no choice but to be cordial to their guests and appear lighthearted. The absence of Aunt Rose, who'd gone to dinner and the ballet with friends, was no coincidence.

To everyone assembled, Tracey must have looked like the perfect chatelaine of the Chappelle manor, dressed in simple black silk for the occasion.

Though the initial conversation had to do with all the girls' teenage school memories, it eventually centered on the adorable triplets and Tracey's marriage to Julien.

At one time or other, every female in the room had had a crush on Angelique's older brother and freely admitted it. Each of the girls had some story to tell about Tracey and how in love she'd been with him, how she'd carried his picture in her wallet long before he'd come home from Cambridge.

But the coup de grace was delivered by Isabelle, who revealed Tracey's deepest secret.

"Do you know what Tracey told me after she blew out all eighteen candles on her birthday cake?" Isabelle confided to Julien so the whole table could hear. "She said she was going to marry you and live here forever. If I recall correctly, she mentioned something about having six handsome sons who would look just like you, *mon cher frère*."

"You've got a good start," Angelique teased while everyone else at the table laughed wholeheartedly.

None of them had any idea of the suffering they caused Tracey, the pain. Averting her eyes, she refused to look at Julien. She could tell by the way his mocking gaze never left her face that he was loving every minute of her sister's candid revelations.

While he allowed the girls to regale him with more tidbits about Tracey's huge crush on him, his calculated silence invited them to go on and on and do their worst damage where she was concerned.

Through the din of excited chatter, she could hear his mind saying to her, *Everyone knows that you've always loved me, that you always will. There's no way I'm letting you give up on our marriage, mon amour.*

All of a sudden, Tracey couldn't stand it any longer. She found herself remembering other meals at this very table with both families present.

How could her mother and Henri have allowed such a thing to happen? Why didn't they intervene before it was too late?

Overwhelmed by intense pain, Tracey proffered the excuse that she needed to use the rest room, then hurried out of the dining hall.

It was just as well she did because when she dashed upstairs to check on the children, she discovered that Valentine was giving the maid problems. One look at her tiny flushed face and Tracey guessed it was her daughter's turn to be sick now that the boys had recovered.

Though she would never wish illness on anyone, least of all her own precious babies, Tracey was relieved that Valentine's condition made it impossible for her to go back downstairs.

It wasn't long before Julien—formally dressed in a midnight blue suit that made him look so handsome it took Tracey's breath—came into the nursery. His long strides shortened the distance in a hurry. "What in the hell is going on, Tracey?"

He so rarely swore, Tracey knew he was really angry. Even Valentine sensed it and clung to Tracey's neck.

"As you can see," she said in a low voice, "Valentine's not well. I thought she looked a little flushed before the party started so I came up to check on her."

Which wasn't altogether a lie, but Tracey had assumed that the crisp fall air had had something to do with the roses in her daughter's cheeks earlier.

Grim-faced, he put a hand on Valentine's forehead. "*Mon Dieu!* She's burning up." One look at his miserable daughter and his black expression turned to one of frustration and concern.

Tracey could read his mind. He'd orchestrated the evening to his advantage, but Valentine's unexpected sickness fell outside his machinations.

Without looking her husband in the eye, Tracey relished telling him, "I'm going to have to get her fever down. Go back to our guests and spend the rest of the evening with them. Please tell them I'm sorry, but Valentine needs me."

In the pregnant pause that followed, she could feel Julien's white-hot tension. "Our daughter may be ill, but she's not the reason you bolted a few minutes ago."

"Please, Julien, you're upsetting her."

He bit out an epithet. "You won't always have the children to wear like a shield against me. This night isn't over yet," he warned fiercely.

She held her breath until he turned on his heel and strode swiftly from the nursery.

The second he was gone, Tracey went limp and clung to her daughter. When she got some of her strength back, she gave the baby liquid aspirin to bring down her temperature, then took her to her room across the hall.

The double bed was big enough to hold both of them comfortably. That way, Valentine wouldn't disturb the boys and Tracey could nurse her daughter without having to keep getting up to check on her.

More than anything else, Tracey needed the comfort of Valentine's warm little body, someone on whom she could lavish her love without it being wrong or forbidden.

Feeling her mother's arms around her must have given Valentine the security she craved. After draining half a bottle of apple juice, she and Tracey both fell asleep.

When Tracey awakened the next morning, she discovered herself alone. Since none of the maids would have disturbed her, it meant that at some point during the night, Julien had come into her bedroom.

She knew exactly why he'd come.

For the past three weeks he'd kept his word and hadn't once tried to make love to her. But tonight had precipitated a situation that was fast growing out of control. Julien was on the verge of snapping.

Even from opposite ends of the huge banquet table, whenever she'd dared look at him, she'd caught glimpses of raw hunger in his eyes. To her horror, her body had leaped in response to that pulsating desire and he knew it!

Tracey hid her face in her hands.

She had the strongest conviction that Julien had come to her in the night because he couldn't help himself.

Thank heavens she'd been asleep!

Thank heavens he'd found Valentine cuddled next to her mother!

But what about the next time, when the children were all well and sleeping soundly in the nursery? When he knew Tracey would be alone?

She shot straight up in bed. *There couldn't be a next time.*

Since Isabelle was leaving on the afternoon plane, Tracey would use Valentine's illness as the excuse to say good-bye at the house.

While Julien ran Isabelle to the airport, Tracey would slip away during the children's naps and get a hotel in town.

Her promise to stay the full month with Julien was no longer important. She had to get out of his house *today*.

CHAPTER NINE

AT LAST all three babies were asleep. Valentine had fussed the most because of her cold, but she'd finally succumbed.

Tracey glanced at her watch. Ten after four. Julien and Rose would be halfway to Geneva with Isabelle and Alex right now. The perfect time for Tracey to go down to the kitchen and enjoy tea with Solange.

When the housekeeper wasn't watching, Tracey would grab for the wallet she'd hidden in one of the drawers and disappear out the back door. By the time anyone discovered she was missing, she'd be safely ensconced in a hotel room with a lock. From there she'd phone the château and enlist Solange's help with the babies until Julien returned.

After one more fleeting glance at her children, Tracey tiptoed across the nursery floor. But she never left the room because she came up against something rock hard that prevented her from going anywhere.

"*Julien*!"

She staggered from the impact but he locked her against his virile body, defeating her.

Her shocked gaze flew to his and what she saw in those black depths caused her body to tremble violently. "W-what are you doing here?"

The wintry smile didn't reach his eyes. "I decided to let Rose drive your sister to the airport so you and I could spend the rest of the afternoon and evening together undisturbed."

Dear God. He knew!

"But Valentine—"

"She's sleeping soundly and the maids are close by."

Tracey's mouth had gone so dry she could hardly make a sound. "I don't think she should be left alone, Julien."

"Really." His lips thinned to a white line of anger. "Then how do you explain *this*?" He reached inside the breast pocket of his shirt and held up her wallet. "I watched you plant it in the kitchen drawer this morning when you thought I was in my study. I know exactly what you're up to, *petite*."

His eyes glittered with rage. "Now that I have proof you've broken the promise you made to me at the clinic, there's no longer any contract between us. After a year's abstinence, I intend to make love to my wife and there isn't a thing you can do about it."

"*No!*" she screamed, but Julien wasn't listening. In a lightning move, he picked her up in his arms. Holding her cruelly tight, he lowered his dark head and covered her mouth with smothering force, reducing her cries to pathetic little moans. Then he started down the hall toward the stairs and Tracey felt the last avenue of escape close over her head.

Julien was a physically powerful man who'd always kept his emotions under control. The only time she'd seen him lose his sangfroid was the night he'd threatened Jacques if he so much as looked at Tracey again. A terrified Jacques had backed off and had never come near her since.

But over the past year, too much damage had been done to Julien and she'd finally unleashed the savage in him. Louise had warned her she could only drive him so far....

By the time they'd reached his suite on the third floor, Tracey had fought him so hard she'd reached the point of exhaustion.

When she felt the mattress against her back, every bit of fight seemed to go out of her. Julien's body all but covered hers so he knew the exact moment she gave up the struggle. That's when he started making love to her in earnest, overwhelming her with his need, pouring out the driving passion he'd had to suppress for so long.

"Stop, Julien!" she screamed when he left her mouth alone long enough to kiss her throat. He'd finally sent her over the edge and there was no going back. "What we're doing is a *sin!*"

For a brief interval, he kept on kissing her perfumed skin, then after a deep chuckle she felt to her toes, he whispered huskily, "We're married, *mon amour*. The only thing sinful about this is how wonderful it feels to be loving again. Is that why you ran away from me? Because you're ashamed of losing yourself in my arms? Are you afraid to admit that this is the place you'd rather be than anywhere else in the world?"

He cupped her hot face in his hands and willed her to answer him.

"Tell me the truth, *mignonne*. No more lies. In some ways, your father had a puritanical outlook on life. Did he teach you that it was sinful for a man and a woman to enjoy each other the way we do?" He shook her gently. "Is that what happened?"

"No..." she groaned aloud, moving her head back and forth as hot tears gushed from her eyes. "He wasn't *my* father, Julien."

Julien went still, then his brows formed into one black slash of consternation. "What are you saying?"

Tracey took a fortifying breath. "Henri Chappelle was my father, too. Yours *and* mine."

Such was Julien's enamored state, he couldn't comprehend what she was telling him. Blinking in confusion he grasped her tighter, though she was certain he was unconscious of his great strength.

Oh, dear God, help me. "You're my half brother, darling," she whispered in a tortured voice. "I'm your half sister. Your father made his confession to me before the priest gave him the last rites."

A wild look crossed Julien's face, creating the illusion that he was part jungle predator. His expression was more terrifying than all her night-mares put together.

"You're lying," he grated through locked teeth, his eyes devoid of light.

"No." She cupped his rigid jaw with her hand, afraid his face had been forever transformed into a cold, lifeless facsimile of itself, just as she'd feared. "He and Mother had an affair after you and Jacques a-and Isabelle were born." Swallowing a sob, she said, "I always wondered where my blond hair came from."

Julien's taut body didn't move. All the while she'd been talking, he'd been trying to grasp every-thing, tearing it apart then putting it back together to find an acceptable answer when there was none—exactly the way she'd been doing for so many months.

His chest heaved in tangible agony. "Do you swear before God you're telling me the truth?"

"Yes, darling. You know I love you more than life itself. I could never lie to you." Trying to stifle her sobs, she said, "Why do you think I ran away? I couldn't bear it."

She saw his throat working. Like an incurable disease, the pain was eating him alive. "Would you swear it before Monseigneur Louvel?"

"Yes."

"*Mon Dieu.*"

His muttered imprecation sounded as if it had come from the lips of a dying man.

For endless minutes, his incredible black eyes probed her soul trying to come up with any other answer than the one she'd just given him.

With tears running down her cheeks and over his hands, she cried, "I wanted to spare you. I'd hoped to run away where you could never find me so that in time you'd learn to hate me and love someone else.

"But when I found out I was pregnant, I had to turn to Rose for help. You know the rest.... Louise told me I suppressed most of my memories to stave off the pain as long as possible."

She heard her name cried on a mournful sound before he crushed her in his arms. They clung to each other in desperation, then came the inevitable silence and the convulsive heaves of his body.

Needing to be strong for him, Tracey absorbed each shudder, recognizing the layers his mind was being forced to wade through before he could accept this new reality.

When he could find words, his voice was barely recognizable. "I know you're not lying, *mignonne*, but I refuse to accept what you've told me until we've spoken to the monseigneur."

"That was the first thing I thought of doing, but then I remembered the confidentiality between a confessor and his priest. The monseigneur would never break his vows, not even if your fa—Henri bared his soul to him."

"He'll tell me," Julien vowed with a violence that made Tracey's heart bleed all over again. "When he understands the gravity of Father's confession to you, the far-reaching consequences to both our families and our children, he'll be forced to reveal what he knows. I'll remind him that his responsibility is to the *living*, not the dead.''

His hands slid to her shoulders, unconsciously squeezing them until she almost moaned from the pressure.

''I don't want to wait to talk to him. We'll drive over to the church *now*.''

When he was in this mood, Tracey knew better than to argue with him or suggest that he call to see if this was a convenient time for the priest to receive visitors.

''Maybe we'd better check on the chil—''

''The children will be fine,'' he broke in with that authoritative tone she'd only ever heard him use with Jacques, or the people at his work when there was a real crisis. ''Solange guards them like a mother hen and would never let anything happen to them.''

She nodded and would have gotten up from the bed but his hands still held her. Their faces were only centimeters apart, their mouths a mere breath away. She knew he wanted to make love to her and never stop. God knew she wanted him in the same way. Nothing had changed for either of them. It never would.

But now Julien had second sight. Together they were forced to share this new burden of knowledge that their religious and cultural values wouldn't allow them to ignore.

At the very last second, another tremendous shudder wracked his powerful body and he checked himself. With a groan she could feel, he got to his feet and raked his hands through his hair, visibly tormented.

Tracey avoided looking at him and almost made it to the door before his arms came around her from behind, dragging her against him. She gasped from the familiar feel of the masculine physique she loved so well.

He buried his face in her hair. "Tell me none of this is true, *mon amour*," he begged with tears in his deep voice. "Tell me we can come back here tonight and love each other the way we did in Tahiti."

His whole soul was reaching out to her now. She had no defense to counteract his kind of pain.

"Julien, don't you think I want to love you in every possible way for the rest of our lives?" she cried. "If it weren't for the children, I'm not sure I could go on living."

Arms of steel bound her even closer to him. "Don't ever say that, *mon amour*," he commanded her in the fiercest tone she'd ever heard. "I have to believe there has been a mistake. You could have misunderstood Father. He had few lucid moments during his last hours. The priest will clear it up and end this torture. Let's go." Cupping her

elbow, he ushered her from the bedroom and down
the hall.

Don't let your hopes blind you, darling. But
Tracey knew from past experience that all the
wishing in the world wouldn't change his determination. He was a fighter. If by any chance she
had misinterpreted Henri's last words, Julien
wouldn't sleep until he'd learned the real truth for
himself.

With a brief word to Solange, they left the
château through the back entrance and got into the
Ferrari.

While they'd been in Julien's room, it had grown
dark out. Switching on the headlights, he headed
for the main road. But he was too intent on his
destination to be cautious. Rose had just turned
the Mercedes onto the grounds of the estate and he
had to slam on his brakes to avoid crashing into
her.

Muttering a curse, he lowered the window and
called out an apology to her but kept on going
without waiting for a response.

Tracey had it in her heart to feel sorry for her
aunt, who was probably aghast at the speed Julien
was traveling. Not only that, she must have wondered why Tracey was in the car when she was supposed to be home nursing Valentine.

Julien's turmoil was such that they didn't talk
during the short ride to town. By the time they'd
arrived at the rectory next to the cathedral, Tracey's
anxiety had reached its peak. Her husband's cer-

tainty that there'd been a mistake had started infecting her.

She found herself offering a fervent prayer that Julien was right, that the priest would have another answer for them, one that would free them from their prison and allow them to continue on in the sanctity of marriage.

"*Je regrette*, Monsieur Chappelle," the caretaker responded after they'd alighted from the car and tugged on the bellpull. "The monseigneur is away in Neuchâtel. If he stays the night, he will phone. All I can do is tell him that you came by and are most anxious to speak to him."

Julien's frustration was so great he almost crushed her hand in his grip. Tracey didn't cry out. In fact, as they turned away and walked back to the car, she welcomed the pain, wishing it could blot out the agony wracking their souls.

The tires screeched against the cobblestones as Julien backed out of the drive and raced through the narrow side street bordering the cathedral.

"Julien," she ventured in a tremulous voice, "after we make certain the children are all right, I think it would be best if I checked into a hotel tonight."

"You're not going anywhere," he ground out, the violence of his tone stunning her into silence. "Aside from what the priest has to say, there are DNA tests we'll have run on ourselves and the children to verify whether or not the same blood flows in our veins.

"But until we know for an absolute certainty that you and I were fathered by the same man, you'll share my bed."

"I can't do that, Julien," she whispered heart-brokenly. "You weren't there to hear your father."

"That's right," he bit out in fury. "More and more I'm finding it inconceivable that he would wait until death's door to keep something so damning from everyone in the family but *you*, or that your father and mother never once hinted at their liaison."

Tracey was listening intently. She'd thought those same thoughts—rehearsed those same arguments—so many times, she'd almost gone insane.

"My father was a cold man, not given to a lot of emotion, but I never knew him to be intentionally cruel. The night Jacques and I almost came to blows, I told Father how I felt about you, that one day I intended to marry you. He had his opportunity to tell me the truth then, *mignonne*, but he never said a word."

"Oh, Julien…" Her voice rang with joy. *Maybe Henri really had been too far gone to make sense.*

"I suppose it's possible he could have been unfaithful to Mother," Julien continued in the same vein. "She was ill for many years, but I always sensed that she was happy in her marriage. She never alluded to a possible affair between him and another woman, let alone your mother."

He shook his head. "After considering every aspect, I have to believe the heavy painkillers caused his rambling, that he didn't have any idea what he was saying.''

"That's because you *want* to believe it!" she cried in renewed fear because his logic was too convincing and she could feel herself weakening.

His dark head whipped around and he impaled her with his eyes. "Don't *you, mon amour*?"

Tracey couldn't lie to him or withstand his laser-like glance. She looked out the window before tearfully confessing, "More than anything."

"Then there's nothing else to discuss. *Mon Dieu*, it's a miracle you're alive and well. Tonight we're going to celebrate your return to life, to me." Another groan escaped. "Do you have any idea how much I need to hold you again, to feel you in my arms all night long?"

By this time they'd reached the private estate road, but before she was even cognizant of it, he'd pulled the car to the side and had reached for her.

"Tracey..." he murmured against her trembling mouth. "I can't wait any longer for this." Then he was igniting passions that turned her body liquid and had her straining toward him in spite of the gearshift being in the way.

Like a starving person who had finally come home to feast, she let go of her reservations and gave herself up to Julien's kiss, unable to fight her love or the clamoring of her senses for the assuagement only her husband could give.

Losing track of time, she sought the exquisite rapture of his mouth and hands, anticipating the intimacy she would share with him once they returned to the house. But they were so on fire for each other, they couldn't break apart long enough for Julien to start up the car. A year's deprivation had rendered them frenzied in their desire to show their love.

When headlights of another car unexpectedly flashed through the rear window, illuminating the interior of the Ferrari, Julien tore his lips from Tracey, cursing the person who dared intrude on his private property this late.

Struggling for breath, Tracey looked around in time to see a black limousine with its official church insignia pull up alongside them.

"*Mon Dieu!*" Julien's voice dropped like rocks. "It's Monseigneur Louvel."

Julien stepped out of the car and the two men held a short conversation. Before she knew it, her husband was back.

"We're going to follow him to the rectory. Under the circumstances, it's just as well no one at the château knows about this meeting."

"I agree. D-did you tell him why we wanted to meet with him?"

"No."

With that one word she had to be satisfied since Julien showed no inclination to talk. She couldn't blame him, not after what had transpired before the priest came on the scene.

Fortunately, the short drive gave her enough time to comb her hair and put on a little makeup. But nothing could restore the ecstasy she'd felt before the priest arrived.

By the time they reached the church grounds and were shown inside the *salon*, Tracey was petrified at what they might learn. Fresh guilt assailed her for having given in to her emotions, no matter how briefly. Julien darted her a private glance that told her to stop torturing herself. They had nothing to fear.

I pray you're right, darling.

Once the monseigneur asked them why they'd come, Julien started in without preamble, then invited Tracey to tell the priest exactly what Henri had said to her moments before he died.

After she'd finished, Julien demanded, "Did my father confess the same thing to you, Father? We've been through a living hell and it's still not over. You are privy to certain information that will affect our lives forever."

While Tracey held her breath, Monseigneur Louvel clapped his hands on his knees and looked Julien straight in the eye. "I commiserate with your pain, and pray God's blessings upon both of you. But a confession is for God and no one else."

Julien sucked in his breath. "Our marriage is sacred!"

The priest nodded. "Yes. And for that reason, there is something I can tell you, but be careful lest you interpret it the wrong way."

His amber eyes switched to Tracey and looked on her with a compassion that struck new terror in her heart.

"Once, years ago, a woman who resembles you strongly came into the chapel to pray. She looked so sad. When I asked if I could be of help, she told me she wasn't a Catholic, but hoped it was all right if she stayed there a while because she felt the need for more spirituality in her life.

"I asked if she wanted to talk to someone. She said it wouldn't help, not if her husband couldn't forgive her. Then she left. I didn't see her again until years later when she accompanied the Chappelle family to mass for Angelique's first communion." He spread his hands. "That is all I know. I'm sorry." He made the sign of the cross and left them alone to talk.

In the ghastly silence that followed, Tracey rose to her feet, traumatized by the priest's words. She didn't need to look at Julien to feel his shocked reaction. What the monseigneur had just told them was as damning as Henri's confession.

The room started to reel. Out of nowhere, Julien was there to save her from falling. With his arm biting into her waist, he helped her out of the rectory to the car. Before closing the passenger door, he cupped her chin in his hand, forcing her to look at him.

"Don't forget the priest's admonition. He warned us not to put the wrong interpretation on his words."

"Stop it, Julien," she cried in anguish. "We have our answer."

His jaw tightened. "I don't think so. I think he was trying to help us without breaking his vows as a priest."

"You're only saying that b-because you don't want to face the truth. I was that way in the beginning. But I've finally come to terms with it."

His eyes glittered dangerously. "You *never* came to terms with it, *mon amour*. Otherwise you wouldn't have let me kiss you senseless tonight."

"What we did was wrong. I wish to God it had never happened." She tried to turn her head away, but his hand kept her from moving.

"You know you don't mean that," he grated.

Tears poured from her eyes. "Please take me home. We left a sick daughter."

After another tension-fraught moment, Julien released her and went around to the driver's side. For the second time that night, he maneuvered the Ferrari back to the château with a speed that took her breath. "Tomorrow we'll make arrangements to go in for DNA tests."

"There's no point, Julien."

"That's what the doctors in San Francisco said when I told them I was having you moved to the specialized head injury clinic here in Lausanne."

Humbled by his faith and that indomitable will of his, she whispered, "I had no idea. You've been too wonderful to me."

"Are you telling me that if our roles had been reversed, you wouldn't have done everything conceivable to bring me out of that coma?" His hand reached out to squeeze her thigh gently. "Tracey?" he prodded in a husky tone.

"You already know the answer to that."

"Then we understand each other."

"I hope so."

She felt his body tauten once more. "What is that supposed to mean?"

Moistening her lips nervously, she said, "Until we know the results of the tests, I'm going to move to an apartment."

"There's no need for that. I swear I won't touch you."

"I made the same promise to myself when I agreed to come home with you for a month. But tonight I broke that promise. It could happen again, only this time it would be with the almost certain knowledge that we're brother and sister. The thought sickens me, Julien. Please. Don't make me despise myself more than I already do."

There was a deadly silence for the rest of the drive home. Once he'd shut off the motor, Tracey tried to get out, but he'd set the lock, making escape impossible.

"Are you telling me that if we find out we have the same father, you're going to live apart from me?"

"Julien, we'll have to get divorced. There's no other solution!" she cried out in torment. "I'll find a place in Chamblandes. That's only two minutes away from you. We can share in the raising of the children so they'll see both of us as much as possible. I'll take care of them while you're at work, and you can come for them whenever you're through. In time, you'll meet s-someone else and be able to—"

"*Mon Dieu*," he cut in abruptly, "I don't believe what I'm hearing."

"That's because you're still in shock. You need sleep."

"After today, that would be impossible."

"Don't..." she begged him in a tortured whisper.

"Be warned, Tracey. Whatever you're thinking, I didn't spend a year of my life getting you back only to let you go again!"

"We'll still be friends, Julien."

"*Friends*?" His angry laugh filled the car's interior.

"Yes, darling. For our children's sake. They say time heals all wounds. I-it's possible you'll want to marry again one day."

"If you can say that to me, then you never knew me." His frigid voice was crucifying her.

"I had months before my accident to face reality."

"Months to have met another man, you mean," he accused hotly and bolted from the car. "Is that why you're flinging marriage in my face, because there's someone else waiting to warm your bed?"

Tracey had never seen Julien this out of control in her life. Everything she'd feared where he was concerned was coming to fruition.

Slowly she got out of the passenger seat. "The children are my one and only priority," she replied quietly. "If you'll support me in that endeavor, that's all I'll ever desire or need."

In the moonlight, his ravaged, gray face chilled her to the bone. Panic-stricken, she hurried into the house.

What a cruel, bitter irony that an accident of birth would forever deny them the comfort of each other's love, the only thing they ever truly wanted out of life.

CHAPTER TEN

"TRACEY? I think I've found the wallpaper for you. Come in the living room and look at this."

"We'll be there in a minute, Aunt Rose. Won't we, my little sweetheart?" Tracey kissed Jules's tummy until he was convulsed with laughter. First came the baby powder, then a clean diaper and a fresh change of T-shirt and overalls.

Finally all three babies were ready for their father to pick up for the weekend. Since that disastrous night three weeks ago when the priest had confirmed Tracey's worst fears, she'd been living in a sort of limbo, with Julien dropping off the children on his way to work and picking them up at the end of the day.

They'd decided to trade off the babies every weekend. This time it was her turn to let the children go. She dreaded it, dreaded the loneliness of her third-floor apartment when the children weren't there. Getting through Friday evening to Monday morning without her darlings was turning out to be the major achievement of her existence.

Rose knew how difficult this time had been for Tracey and had agreed to come over and spend the night to keep her company. She was the one who had suggested that some redecorating would help

Tracey feel more at home in the gracious three-bedroom apartment Julien had found for her.

Only three minutes from the château, the security and privacy were rivaled only by the charm of the rooms facing the lake. Tracey didn't care that they needed refurbishing, but recognized that Rose wanted to feel useful.

So far there'd been no word about the results of the DNA tests done on the five of them. The doctor said it might be another couple of weeks before they heard anything. Tracey tried not to think about it since they'd only confirm what she already knew.

No matter how devastating this time had been for them, she was thankful Julien hadn't fought the separation. At least a routine of sorts had been established. Soon the children would come to view both the apartment and the château as home.

Neither she nor Julien wanted anyone on either side of the family to know the real reason they'd separated, not even Rose. There'd been enough pain to last a lifetime. One careless word could harm their children someday, something they'd fight to avoid.

By tacit agreement, they kept their conversation limited to talk of the babies. They never discussed how he spent the hours away from her, or what she did to pass the time when her day wasn't full of feedings and baths.

Out of a sense of self-preservation, she never looked into her husband's eyes. To any passerby, she and Julien probably appeared to be old acquaintances who were civil and polite to each other, nothing more.

It killed Tracey to see the new remoteness in Julien these days. He'd grown a hard veneer that changed him into an emotionless replica of his former self. Only when he responded to the children did she detect traces of the vital man she loved with her whole soul.

She didn't even want to think what their lives would be like if they didn't have their precious babies who were fast growing into little people with minds and personalities all their own.

Julien was probably on his way over right now, anxious to cuddle Valentine and play with the boys. Tracey yearned to get right into the thick of it with them. Every time she found herself daydreaming, she chastised herself for losing control and tried to concentrate on something else. But it was a futile exercise when she was so madly in love with him.

"Who was on the phone?" she asked her aunt as she walked into the living room carrying Jules. She'd heard it ring but knew Rose would answer it.

"Julien. He's going to be late."

Tracey bit her lip as a dichotomy of emotions attacked her. Though relieved because she'd have the children a little longer, she lived for his visits, no matter how brief.

"Did he say why?"

"A business dinner, I believe."

"At the house?"

"No. The Château D'Ouchy."

"I see." Tracey tried to keep her voice level, but failed miserably and her aunt knew it. When Julien left the house for the evening, that meant there would be women as well as men in his dining party.

Tracey had never thought of herself as a jealous person, but that was before Julien had become forbidden to her. From here on out he was fair game to any female in sight. One too many times a beautiful woman would make a play for him on an evening not unlike this, and he'd respond....

Just the thought of it ripped Tracey's heart out.

"Dear?" Rose called to her in a worried voice. "Are you all right?"

"Yes. Of course," Tracey hastened to assure her aunt. "I was thinking that the babies' sweaters are too hot. I'll take them off until he comes."

After relieving the other two of their outer garments, she put all three tots together in the playpen, then crawled around on the floor playing peekaboo with them through the mesh.

One by one, the children laughed belly laughs that were so contagious, Rose had to wipe the tears from her eyes.

"Oh, Tracey. You're a natural mother. They absolutely adore you."

"I hope so, because they're my whole life."

Rose's expression sobered. "Why can't you include Julien in that statement?"

One mention of her husband and the happiness Tracey had been feeling as she cavorted with her children shriveled up.

"We've been over that ground before, Rose. Why don't we change the subject? Have you heard from Iz?"

"Not since you have. Julien suggested they consult a good financial adviser and I think she's talked Bruce into it. It's a start in the right direction. Maybe the day will come when she'll begin to concentrate on being the kind of mother you are."

"I thought she handled Alex extremely well for being four months pregnant," Tracey defended.

"But it doesn't come naturally to her. She needs to watch you."

Tracey frowned. "You're serious, aren't you?"

"Perfectly. She treats him like an expensive toy that has to be handled carefully. She picks him up and puts him down, but she doesn't get into a mad scramble with him as we used to say when I was a young woman. She doesn't get physical with him the way you do with your children. Your father used to play with you like that. That's probably where you learned it."

"*Daddy*?"

Rose blinked. "Of course. The first thing he'd do when he came home from work was make a beeline for you. You'd both get down on the floor and play hard until your mother called him to dinner."

"What about Iz?"

"I'm afraid she was your mother's girl."

Tracey shook her head. "That's terrible. There should never be a mommy's girl and a daddy's girl. Each child should feel loved in the same way."

"You see, darling? You have a true mother's instincts, but some parents aren't blessed in the same way." A shadow of pain crossed her aunt's face, one that haunted Tracey. "And sometimes, circumstances change the nature of things."

There was such sadness in Rose's remark, Tracey felt her aunt was trying to tell her something. She broke out in a cold sweat.

Did Rose knew the truth?

Tracey stared at her aunt. "You're not talking in generalities, are you?"

"No. I'm talking about your parents because they're not here to defend themselves and I'm afraid my reminiscing about the past has given you some wrong impressions."

"You mean about my parents showing their preferences for me and Iz?"

"Exactly."

Tracey's heart bled to think of the man she'd always thought of as her father trying so hard to love another man's child. Without stopping to think, Tracey blurted, "I already know the reason why, Aunt Rose."

The older woman let out a quiet gasp but Tracey heard her.

"How long have you known?" she asked in a shocked voice.

"A year."

"Who told you?"

"My father."

"But he said he wasn't going to tell you until you were married and had a child of your own."

"That's exactly what he did do, except that neither he, nor I, knew that I was pregnant at the time."

"Tracey—you're not making sense. Your parents were killed in that plane crash long before you married Julien."

Totally confused, Tracey said, "Now you're the one not making sense since we both know Henri Chappelle is my biological father."

"Oh, no, Tracey. No!" Rose cried and leaped to her feet in agitation. "Whatever gave you that idea?"

Tracey started to shake and couldn't stop. "I went in to see Henri for a few minutes on the day he died. H-he told me about his affair with mother, how they decided that she and Daddy would raise the baby so no one would ever know the truth. He begged me not to tell Julien because it would hurt him. Then he wept and reached for my hand, murmuring that he loved me like a daughter. I thought I heard him say something about forgiving him, but his words became garbled. I was in a state of shock when I left the room."

"Oh, no," Rose whispered, shaking her head. "You thought that baby was *you*! *That's* why you ran away, why you fought so hard to end your marriage. Oh, my dearest girl. Don't you know he was talking about Isabelle?"

Tracey felt the blood drain out of her face. *"Isabelle?"*

"Yes, Tracey. Yes. Isabelle is Henri's daughter, not you. If you'll think about it, she has Henri's eyes and bone structure. I'm surprised you never noticed. Your sister was conceived during a time when your parents were estranged."

"What?" Tracey was too staggered to respond.

"Soon after their marriage, your mother suffered a miscarriage. Your father was so upset by her depression, he didn't want to try for another baby in case history repeated itself. She interpreted it that he didn't love her anymore.

"On one of their trips to Lausanne, she got too close to Henri because he and Celeste were having problems. Her arthritis unintentionally caused her to shut him out, making him vulnerable. Your mother told me they were only together one time, but Isabelle was the result."

"This is all so unbelievable," Tracey cried out, aghast.

"It was very sad. Your mother confessed everything to your father and he forgave her because he knew he hadn't been attentive to her when she needed him. But he insisted on raising Isabelle as his own daughter to prevent a scandal. He agreed they should tell her one day after she married. And though he tried, he could never love her the way he loved you."

"Did Celeste know?"

"Yes, and guilt made her feel partly responsible."

"How horrible for everyone."

"Yes," Rose murmured pensively. "After that, your father unconsciously lavished most of his attention on you. To compensate, your mother doted on Isabelle. But when Jacques made your life so miserable, your father's bitterness flared up and he put an end to the family trips, with the exception that he allowed Isabelle to visit Angelique for a few weeks each year out of compassion for Henri."

"So *Daddy* was the reason.... It's all making sense. Does Isabelle know the truth now?"

"No. Not yet. One day I'll tell her when the time is right."

"Then I don't understand why Henri said those things to me."

"He assumed your parents had already told you about Isabelle. Henri was asking for your forgiveness because he was aware of your love for Julien and knew it had broken your heart to be parted from him. He was afraid you blamed him for the separation."

I did, her heart moaned with remembered pain.

"Oh, Aunt Rose..." Tracey's whole body trembled. "What you've just told me has made me the happiest woman on earth. *Julien and I aren't related*!" she shouted for joy, bringing the children's heads around.

Her beloved little offsprings stared at her as if she was a complete oddity, making her want to laugh and cry all at the same time.

Their perfect children. Hers and Julien's. Able to grow up with the expectation of normal lives.

Rose grinned. "Oh, yes, you are related, but only by your own marriage, *which* your husband refused to give up on. Of that, I am living proof! Honestly, Tracey, I never saw a man so in love with a woman in my life."

Tracey's euphoria made her feel she was going to burst. "I—I've got to go to him! I've got to find him right now! I've got to tell him! Aunt Rose—"

"I'm planning on tending the babies through the weekend," she said, anticipating her niece's request with the greatest of joy. "Put on that beautiful violet dress he bought to complement your lovely hair. But don't keep him waiting too long! After the agony he has suffered, another minute would be too cruel.

"Oh, Tracey dear, how I'd love to see the look in his eyes when you join him at dinner and release him from that terrible prison...."

Tracey was living for that moment herself.

The next hour flew by. While Rose called the Château D'Ouchy to ascertain that Julien was still there with his dinner guests, Tracey showered and washed her hair in record time.

Fastening her amethyst-jeweled earrings, she slipped into high heels with matching jewels on the straps, then pronounced herself ready to meet her husband. After a kiss to her babies' rounded cheeks and a huge hug to her aunt, Tracey dashed down to the waiting taxi Rose had called for her.

She was so excited and jittery she couldn't have driven a car and was thankful to be chauffeured to the elegant château-hotel located in the lakeside suburb of Ouchy.

Judging by her hot cheeks, Tracey knew she was glowing when she entered the hotel and asked directions for the Chappelle party. The *maître d'hotel* couldn't help but hear her heart thudding out of control.

Unaware of heads turning, she wound her way through the main floor dining area, her gilt hair falling from a side part as it swayed freely about her shoulders.

She felt seventeen again and hopelessly, painfully in love with the handsome man she spied seated at the head table in the private dining room.

Julien looked marvelous in anything he wore, but never more spectacular than when he was turned out in full dress tux. Tonight the black of his jacket accented his olive complexion and emphasized his striking male features in a way that made her breath catch.

Even at the tender age of seventeen, the chemistry between them had been potent. Six years later and Tracey was still reacting the same way. She always would.

For a brief moment, she hung back to savor her joy. After twelve months of pain, she could drink her fill of her husband without any accompanying guilt. The freedom to love him completely was a gift beyond comprehension.

He hadn't seen her yet. Paul Loti, the comptroller of Chappelle House, held Julien's attention with something of vital import. Their two heads were bent together in concentration, one carrot red, the other a familiar black. Almost jumping out of her skin with anticipation, Tracey advanced toward her husband.

Suddenly the room grew quiet. One by one Julien's employees and their spouses recognized her and stopped talking to smile at her and nod a welcoming greeting. On some level, Julien must have detected a change in the room's ambience because his head lifted abruptly and swerved around.

The second his intelligent eyes caught sight of her chiffon-clad figure, the way the material swished around her long, slender legs, he leaped to his feet and started toward her.

Paul had the foresight to catch his chair, which would surely have crashed to the parquetry flooring, but her husband never noticed.

A mixture of emotions played across his unforgettable face, robbing his complexion of color. As he drew closer, she saw shock, because never once since she'd come out of her coma had she sought him out, or initiated a visit to his office.

Only a few feet away now, she divined fear. After everything she'd done to make certain they stayed apart, he had to assume that her unprecedented appearance at his company dinner meant something must be seriously wrong with one of the children, or perhaps all of them.

Yet underlying his surprise and anxiety was a look of incredulity. She knew he was seeing the *old* Tracey. His bride. The starry-eyed lover of those warm Tahitian nights who'd given him her body, her heart, her soul...

"*Tracey* ..."

There was a tentativeness in his low, husky voice as he whispered her name. For the first time since she'd known him, he sounded unsure of himself. The fear that this might be some fantastic dream from which he would awaken more desolate than before, seemed to rob him of the decisiveness she'd always associated with his character. For Julien to be uncertain of anything was a revelation to her.

With a compulsion too strong to be denied, she reached for him.

In that one act, she conveyed something more powerful than words. She conjured up the magic that unlocked the door of his prison.

When he intercepted her hand midair and clung to it, Tracey knew he'd divined the truth. Explanations could come later.

Like a miracle, his taut body relaxed. She felt him let go of the anger and pain, felt him shed the layers of unbridled grief as if they'd never been.

A brilliant smile illuminated her countenance, turning her eyes into orbs of green fire. They stared into the stunning blackness of his with pure, unadulterated joy, savoring the glory of this moment, the promise of future glories.

Then, with the confidence born of a woman who knew she was loved, who knew that she and she alone had the right and privilege to claim this one perfect man for her own, she turned to face their captive audience.

"Chers amis—" her voice caught a little *"—*please forgive the interruption, but I have something of vital importance to discuss with my husband in private.

"B-because of me, he's been under a tremendous strain this past year. Through it all, I'm well aware of how supportive and patient you've been. Thank you for helping Julien handle an impossible situation.

"As my repayment, I'll make you a promise that from here on out, everything is going to be different. If you'll give us a few days to enjoy a second honeymoon, I'll send him back a new man."

At first there was complete silence. Then Paul started to clap. He was followed by the people at the head table. Soon everyone in the room was standing and applauding.

"Make that a few weeks," Julien amended wickedly before pulling a flushed Tracey toward the exit. To the delight of his staff, she almost had to run to keep up with him. No one could be in any doubt that the head of Chappelle House had other thoughts on his mind than business.

Tracey assumed Julien was headed for the exit to the parking lot. She didn't understand when he stopped at the front desk with his arm clamped around her waist. "We would like a room, please. Preferably the bridal suite."

The correct-looking concierge flashed them a subtle smile. *"Certainement*, Monsieur Chappelle. With our compliments."

Tracey hid her face in her husband's broad shoulder. "The château is only a few minutes away. There's no nee—"

"There's every need," he contradicted her, brushing his lips against the adorable rosebud mouth lifted to him with unknowing provocation. "You've put me in such a condition, I'm not capable of moving a meter, let alone the distance to the car. *Tu comprends, mon amour*?"

The concierge must have heard Julien because when he handed him the key, he murmured, "Your elevator is the one you can see on your right. Do you require assistance?"

"Only my wife's." He chuckled. With his arm still hugging her against him, they crossed the lobby to their own private elevator, one of the best features of the hotel. The second the door closed, he cupped her face in his hands, pressing kisses to her hair, eyes, nose, cheeks and throat. "I feel like I'm dreaming. Tell me, *mignonne*," he said, his voice shaking, "did the doctor call with the results of the DNA tests?"

"No," she whispered, chasing his lips until she found them. "I was given something much better. My source is infallible."

He sucked in his breath. "Does that mean Monseigneur Louvel broke his silence?"

"No, darling. *Aunt Rose*. She verified that your father and my mother had an affair. But it's Isabelle who's your half sister."

"*Isabelle*?" he said her name as the doors opened. He seemed to stagger for a moment. Tracey clung to him, offering him her strength.

"Yes, darling. Now that I know the truth, I understand even better why you've always been able to reach Iz when no one else could."

Julien shook his head, dazed. Slowly they entered the living room. He sank into the nearest couch, pulling Tracey onto his lap. They wrapped their arms around each other in that old, familiar way with Julien burying his face in her hair.

It was like coming home after being lost for years and years in a dark wilderness.

His deep voice murmured, "Monseigneur Louvel warned us there could be another explanation."

"Yes." Tears filled her eyes. "You were right. In his own way, he tried to give us hope."

Julien pulled her closer. "Tell me everything, *mon amour*. Don't leave anything out."

Tracey didn't need her husband's prompting. The desire to share their parents' secret had her pouring out one revelation after another. For an emotion-packed half hour, she supplied him with the sad facts surrounding Isabelle's conception.

"When I think how hard I've been on Jacques..." Julien whispered in a tormented voice.

"No more than I on your father. Before Aunt Rose said anything, I always had this feeling he didn't like me. I was so hurt when he allowed Isabelle to go back to Lausanne for visits."

Julien's hands twisted convulsively in her hair. "Neither of us realized your father was the one responsible. He always seemed to distance himself from me. That was why I never allowed my relationship with you to get physical.''

Tracey shot straight up. ''You mean Daddy was the reason you never kissed me?''

''That's right, *petite*. I meant to marry you and refused to do anything to jeopardize my plans. When he questioned my motives in picking you up from school every day and taking you to my office, I told him I had appointed myself your guardian against Jacques, which was true. Just not the whole truth. I gave him my word that he could trust me to treat you like a cherished sister.''

''Julien . . .'' She hid her face.

''You *should* be blushing,'' he teased softly. ''Never has any man had to withstand more temptation than I.''

''Oh, darling—'' Tracey burrowed closer ''—when I think how I threw myself at you.''

''You did.'' He kissed her neck. ''You were shameless and I adored you. And as long as your love kept growing, as long as those incredible green eyes kept making me feel immortal, I vowed I could be patient long enough for your father to accept me as a son-in-law. Unfortunately, he died before I could talk to him, but now that I know the truth, I doubt he would have given me his blessing.''

''Yes, he would have,'' Tracey returned fervently. ''He was very much aware you were—are my *raison d'être*. He knew what a wonderful man you were or he would never have entrusted me to your care. Daddy and I were very close. I *know* he wouldn't have stood in the way of my happiness.''

Julien embraced her more fully. ''Perhaps not, but I would always have been a reminder of his pain. Father betrayed your father's trust in a way that no man could forgive. I suppose he paid the price for that moment of weakness all the days of his life.''

''I'm sure Mother did, too. But it's over now.''

''Not quite. Isabelle has to be told.''

''Aunt Rose wants to tell her when the time is right. I think she should be the one. She and Mother were extremely close. She'll be able to explain things in a way that Iz will understand and accept.'' Tracey outlined his mouth with her finger. ''When she learns that you're her half brother, she'll love you more than ever. You were always her favorite person, too.''

Julien grasped her hand and kissed the palm. ''After we go back to the château, I'll phone Jacques in Brussels and ask him to come home. We'll invite Angelique over and break the news to them together. It's time we were a family again.''

''I want that more than anything. The pain we've all had to endure because of our parents' affair should have been buried with them. Thank heaven the truth is out at last.''

''Thank heaven you lived through that accident,'' Julien cried in a shaken voice. ''*Mon Dieu*, when I think how close I came to losing you...''

Tracey kissed the tears from his cheeks. ''There was no chance of that. Not with you watching over me and our babies. I'm the most blessed woman alive, Julien Chappelle," she spoke the words against his mouth. "Thank you for never giving up. Thank you for being the kind of man you are, for being father and mother to the children during such a traumatic period in our lives.

"Now it's my turn to take care of you. For the rest of the time granted to us, I'm planning to spend every minute, every second showing you exactly what you mean to me. I love you so much I can't contain it any longer.

"Julien," she cried in an anxious voice, "do you think a person could die from feeling too much love?"

"There's only one way to find out," came his impassioned response as he carried her into the bedroom. "At least if we go up in flames, it will be together, *mon amour*. One thing I can promise you. Wherever our love takes us, *we've only just begun*."

Free Gift Offer

With a Free Gift proof-of-purchase
from any Harlequin® book, you can receive
a beautiful cubic zirconia pendant.

This stunning marquise-shaped stone is a genuine cubic
zirconia—accented by an 18" gold tone necklace.
(Approximate retail value $19.95)

Send for yours today...
compliments of 🔷 HARLEQUIN®

To receive your free gift, a cubic zirconia pendant, send us one original proof-of-
purchase, photocopies not accepted, from the back of any Harlequin Romance®,
Harlequin Presents®, Harlequin Temptation®, Harlequin Superromance®, Harlequin
Intrigue®, Harlequin American Romance®, or Harlequin Historicals® title available in
February, March or April at your favorite retail outlet, together with the Free Gift
Certificate, plus a check or money order for $1.65 U.S./$2.15 CAN. (do not send cash) to
cover postage and handling, payable to Harlequin Free Gift Offer. We will send you the
specified gift. Allow 6 to 8 weeks for delivery. Offer good until April 30, 1997, or while
quantities last. Offer valid in the U.S. and Canada only.

Free Gift Certificate

Name: _____

Address: _____

City: _____ State/Province: _____ Zip/Postal Code: _____

Mail this certificate, one proof-of-purchase and a check or money order for postage
and handling to: HARLEQUIN FREE GIFT OFFER 1997. In the U.S.: 3010 Walden
Avenue, P.O. Box 9071, Buffalo NY 14269-9057. In Canada: P.O. Box 604, Fort Erie,
Ontario L2Z 5X3.

FREE GIFT OFFER   084-KEZ
ONE PROOF-OF-PURCHASE
To collect your fabulous FREE GIFT, a cubic zirconia pendant, you must include this
original proof-of-purchase for each gift with the properly completed Free Gift Certificate.

Take 4 bestselling love stories FREE

Plus get a FREE surprise gift!

Special Limited-time Offer

Mail to Harlequin Reader Service®

3010 Walden Avenue
P.O. Box 1867
Buffalo, N.Y. 14240-1867

YES! Please send me 4 free Harlequin Romance® novels and my free surprise gift. Then send me 6 brand-new novels every month, which I will receive months before they appear in bookstores. Bill me at the low price of $2.67 each plus 25¢ delivery and applicable sales tax if any*. That's the complete price and a savings of over 10% off the cover prices—quite a bargain! I understand that accepting the books and gift places me under no obligation ever to buy any books. I can always return a shipment and cancel at any time. Even if I never buy another book from Harlequin, the 4 free books and the surprise gift are mine to keep forever.

116 BPA A3UK

Name	(PLEASE PRINT)	
Address	Apt. No.	
City	State	Zip

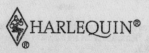